nickelodeon
SpongeBob SquarePants

THE ADVENTURES OF
MAN SPONGE
AND BOY PATRICK

IN THE MEGA JUSTICE COLLECTION

ILLUSTRATED BY THE ARTIFACT GROUP

Random House 🏠 New York

CONTENTS

Published in the United States by Random House
Children's Books, a division of Random House, Inc.,
1745 Broadway, New York, NY 10019, and in Canada
by Random House of Canada Limited, Toronto.

Originally published as three separate titles by Simon
Spotlight Publishing, a division of Simon & Schuster, Inc.:
Goodness, Man Ray!, in 2011; *What Were You Shrinking?*, in
2011; and *E.V.I.L. vs. The I.J.L.S.A.*, in 2012.

created by

Stephen Hillenburg

randomhouse.com/kids
ISBN 978-0-449-81827-5
Printed in the United States of America
10 9 8 7 6 5 4 3 2 1

GOODNESS, MAN RAY!

By David Lewman

DUTY CALLS

SpongeBob pounded on Patrick's rock. "Patrick! Come on! It's time!"

His buddy's house flipped open with Patrick attached. He looked sleepy. "Time for what?" he mumbled. "A nap?"

"No!" SpongeBob said, shaking his head. "Time for us to visit . . . THE MERMALAIR!"

Patrick looked excited. "Oh yeah!" He hopped down and slammed his house shut. "I remember everything now! Except for two things: What's the Mermalair and why are we going there?"

As they hurried along the sidewalk together, SpongeBob reminded Patrick that the Mermalair was the supersecret headquarters of Bikini Bottom's boldest (and oldest) superheroes: Mermaidman and his faithful sidekick, Barnacleboy!

"They're going on vacation to Leisure Village," SpongeBob explained. "And while they're gone, you and I get to take care of the Mermalair!"

Patrick stopped in his tracks. "That sounds like an awfully big job," he said. "Too big for you and me."

SpongeBob nodded. "You might be right, Patrick." He rubbed his chin, thinking hard. Then he snapped his fingers. "But it's not too big of a job for . . .

MAN SPONGE AND BOY PATRICK!

"Who are they?" asked Patrick, puzzled. "Are you sure they're available?"

SpongeBob chuckled. "Yes, I'm sure," he said. Then he lowered his voice to a whisper. "Because Man Sponge and Boy Patrick are you and me!"

"Oh boy!" Patrick said, grinning. "Which one am I?"

As SpongeBob explained who was who, the two best friends rushed out to the edge of Bikini Bottom. Eventually they arrived at a rock wall. It looked smooth, but if you examined it closely,

you could see the outline of a door cleverly hidden in the stone.

"This is it!" SpongeBob cried. "The secret entrance to the secret Mermalair, where Mermaidman and Barnacleboy secretly keep all their hidden secrets!"

Patrick stared at the rock wall. "How do we get in?"

SpongeBob looked around to see if anyone was listening. When he was sure the coast was clear, he put his hand up to his mouth and whispered, "Well, Boy Patrick, the secret to getting inside the Mermalair was personally entrusted to me, Man Sponge, by none other than Mermaidman himself!"

"Wow!" Patrick said, impressed.

"The secret is," SpongeBob continued, "we ring the doorbell."

"Brilliant, Man Sponge!"

SpongeBob rang the doorbell.

BING BONG!

They waited impatiently. Inside, the two aging superheroes made their way to the entrance. When the rock door slid open, SpongeBob and Patrick leaped inside, saluting.

"Man Sponge . . . ," SpongeBob shouted.

"And Boy Patrick . . . ," Patrick added.

"REPORTING FOR DUTY!" they yelled together.

"Yeah, yeah," Barnacleboy said, closing the door behind them. "Follow me."

GREAT WALL OF GADGETS

Barnacleboy led SpongeBob and Patrick deeper into the shadowy cave. Mermaidman, who'd fallen asleep standing by the front door, suddenly awoke and cried out,

"EEEEVVVILLLLL!!!"

As they walked past dripping stalactites and lumpy stalagmites, SpongeBob saw strange, glowing computers and bizarre crime-fighting contraptions. He was so excited, he could barely bring himself to concentrate on what Barnacleboy was saying.

"Now, we want you boys to keep an eye on the place," Barnacleboy explained. "Water the plants and make sure—"

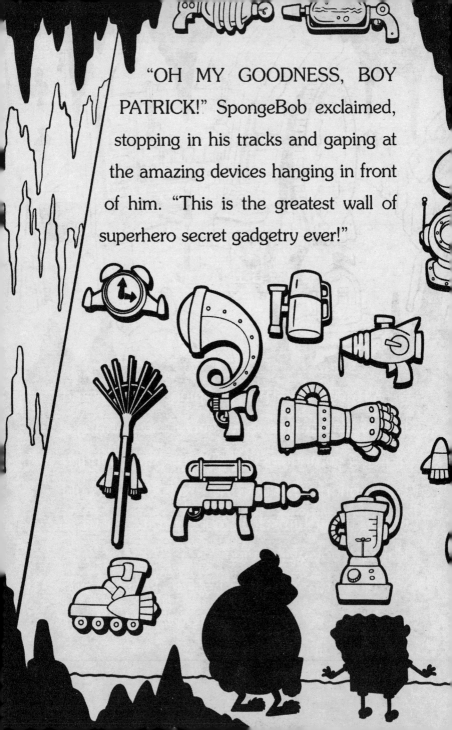

"OH MY GOODNESS, BOY PATRICK!" SpongeBob exclaimed, stopping in his tracks and gaping at the amazing devices hanging in front of him. "This is the greatest wall of superhero secret gadgetry ever!"

It was a wall covered in weird tools and appliances. SpongeBob couldn't wait to get his hands on the astonishing objects he'd heard about in Mermaidman's adventures. "I'm gonna play with the Cosmic Ray!" he sang out.

"I get the Aqua Glove!" Patrick called.

They rushed toward the wall of gadgets, but Mermaidman leaped in front of them, blocking the way. "Hold on there, boys!" he cried. "You cannot play with this stuff!"

SpongeBob backed off, but turned toward a white ball on top of a brass pole. "What about the Orb of Confusion?" he asked, flipping its switch from off to on.

Odd waves passed through the air, like ripples spreading from a rock thrown in water. SpongeBob immediately felt very confused. He stuck out his tongue and rolled his eyes. "DOY! DOYEEE! DUUHHHH!"

Mermaidman quickly turned off the orb. "No!" he gasped. "Prolonged exposure to the Orb of Confusion will give you, uh, confusion!"

SpongeBob snapped out of his state of confusion and grinned. "Of course!" he said. "I remember the Orb of Confusion from one of your greatest adventures, when you captured Man Ray!"

"How did that one go?" asked Mermaidman, scratching his head.

Patrick spoke up. "Man Ray was a bad guy and you wanted to stop the bad guys, so you stopped him!" Patrick was proud of his splendid retelling of the story.

"Doesn't ring a bell," murmured Mermaidman.

SpongeBob pointed to the Orb of Confusion but didn't touch it this time. "You put the Orb of Confusion right outside the vault in the First Nautical Bank. Then you tricked Man Ray into thinking he had to flip the orb's switch to get into the vault and steal all the money."

Patrick interrupted. "Were Man Sponge and Boy Patrick there to help?"

"Of course!" SpongeBob answered. "They helped lure Man Ray into the trap!"

Barnacleboy shook his head. "I don't remember that part."

"Then what happened in the story, Mommy?" Mermaidman asked, a little confused.

"With the help of Man Sponge and Boy Patrick, you captured the evil Man Ray!" SpongeBob said. Patrick clapped his hands. "Good story! Again! Again!"

Barnacleboy picked up his suitcase and headed for the door. "We don't have time for any more stories. Remember, don't touch anything! Especially the Invisible Boatmobile!"

Mermaidman followed his sidekick. "Up, up, and away!" He waddled out of the Mermalair, carrying his luggage.

SpongeBob turned to Patrick, vibrating with excitement. "Just think, Boy Patrick!" he said. "Now WE'RE in charge!"

OH, TARTAR SAUCE!

SpongeBob struck a manly pose. "Come, Boy Patrick! While our heroes are away, we will keep evil at bay!"

He jumped deeper into the cave, flipping and making karate sounds.

Patrick followed, kicking the air with his pink legs.

But as he turned a corner in the cave, Patrick spotted something that made him freeze in his tracks. Trembling, he tried to tell SpongeBob what he saw. "M-m-m-m-m . . ."

SpongeBob heard Patrick and came back to where he stood, shaking with fear. "What is it, trusted sidekick?" he asked.

Patrick still couldn't get out the words. "M-m-m-m . . ."

SpongeBob peered into a cavernous chamber and saw what had frightened Patrick. Shuddering, he couldn't get out the words either. "M-m-m-m . . ."

They clung to each other, terrified. Finally they managed to force out the words they'd been trying to say to each other.

"MAN RAY!!!"

The evil supervillain stood in a dark room, stretching his gloved hands toward SpongeBob and Patrick.

"AAAHH!!"

they screamed, dashing away.

SpongeBob realized Man Ray wasn't chasing them. He tiptoed back to meet Patrick. "How come he's not chasing us, Man Sponge?" Patrick asked.

Man Sponge decided he needed to investigate further. He took a deep breath to calm himself and crept toward Man Ray. The villain stood absolutely still, not making a sound.

"Looks like he's frozen or something, Boy Patrick."

Patrick shivered, muttering, "Fro-fro-fro-fro-fro-fro . . ."

Man Sponge fearlessly approached Man Ray, until he could see that the villain was inside a column of cold, white goo. Knocking on the column, he said, "It appears to be some sort of prison chamber . . ."—he licked the goo—"made out of frozen tartar sauce!"

SpongeBob stood back admiring the tartar-sauce trap. "This is incredible! Next to the Dirty Bubble, the evil Man Ray is the all-time greatest arch-nemesis of Mermaidman and Barnacleboy. I have so many questions to ask him!"

At that very moment, the tartar sauce holding Man Ray started to melt. Laughing goofily, Patrick stood by a control switch he had flipped from FREEZE to UNFREEZE.

SpongeBob ran over to Patrick. "Pat, what are you doing? We're not supposed to touch anything!"

Patrick looked puzzled. "But you said you had a question."

"We could get in trouble!" SpongeBob cried.

"That's not a question," answered Patrick.

While they argued, the tartar sauce melted down past Man Ray's head. His eyes glowed a menacing red.

"They said not to touch anything, and that includes unfreezing a supervillain," SpongeBob insisted.

Then, from above their heads, came a low, evil voice. "I'm FREE!" it gloated, laughing a horrible laugh!

FREE TO LAUGH

"Actually, Mr. Man Ray, sir," SpongeBob pointed out, "only your head is free." The white goo had only melted down to Man Ray's shoulders.

Man Ray looked down and saw that it was true. He was still trapped. "By the supreme authority of wickedness," he growled, "I, the evil Man Ray, command you to release me from this frozen prison at once!"

SpongeBob twiddled his fingers nervously. "Well, Mr. Evil Man Ray, sir, we can't do that."

"WHY NOT?" Man Ray roared. The force

of his powerful voice blew SpongeBob and Patrick back on their heels.

SpongeBob frowned and pointed at Man Ray accusingly. "Because you're EVIL!"

Man Ray thought a moment. Then he spoke, more gently this time. "You mean if I was *good* you'd let me go?"

"Yeah, sure. Why not?" SpongeBob said, shrugging his shoulders. Patrick nodded.

Man Ray saw his chance for escape. "In that case," he said in as friendly a voice as he could manage, "I *am* good!"

SpongeBob's eyes opened wide. "Really?"

Man Ray nodded. "Yes, really."

"Really really?" SpongeBob asked.

"Yes, really really," Man Ray answered, slightly annoyed.

"Really really really?" SpongeBob asked.

"YES, YES ALREADY! I'M GOOD! I'M GOOD!" Man Ray shouted. "Now let me out of here or you'll suffer dire consequences!"

SpongeBob turned to Patrick and shrugged. "Well, that's good enough for me!" He grabbed the big switch and pulled it all the way down from FREEZE to UNFREEZE.

The white goo thawed quickly, starting at the top, around Man Ray's shoulders, and melting down past his feet until he was completely free. He fell to his knees on the ground and looked up with an evil glint in his eyes.

"You fools!" he sneered. "Prepare to be eradicated!"

Man Ray leaped toward SpongeBob and Patrick, but in midair he grabbed his stomach and started to laugh. He fell to the ground, laughing helplessly and clutching his stomach. Smiling, SpongeBob walked up to him with a remote control in his hand.

The belt around Man Ray's waist was vibrating, tickling him mercilessly. "What is this infernal contraption?" he managed to gasp between laughs.

Looking sly, SpongeBob pointed toward the helpless Man Ray. "Don't play dumb, Man Ray! You know that's the Tickle Belt that Mermaidman used on you in Episode Seventeen!"

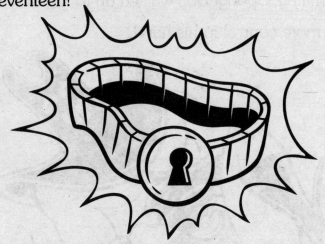

"Oh, I LOVE that episode!" Patrick said.

Man Ray kept laughing as the belt kept tickling him.

"Remember how Mermaidman tricked Man Ray into putting on the belt by telling him it would match his costume perfectly?" SpongeBob asked.

"Oh yeah!" Patrick said. "But didn't Mermaidman get a lot of help from Man Sponge and Boy Patrick?"

"I think you're right, Patrick!" SpongeBob said, grinning.

"That's not the way I remember it," Man Ray said, still giggling and guffawing.

While SpongeBob and Patrick chattered away about their adventures as Man Sponge and Boy Patrick, Man Ray thought to himself, *I need an evil plan that will trick them into taking this belt off me. Time for those acting lessons to pay off!*

GOODNESS LESSON #1

"Oh, boo-hoo! Oh, sob! Oh, cry!" Man Ray wailed.

SpongeBob and Patrick stopped talking and looked at Man Ray, puzzled. Why was he crying?

"Oh, woe is me! You don't know what it's like, being evil for so long!" Man Ray raised his fist in the air dramatically. "Oh, how I wish to be good! If only some kind heroes would show me the path to decency!"

SpongeBob gasped with excitement and turned toward Patrick. "Did you hear that? 'Kind heroes'!"

Patrick nodded. "This is a job for . . ."

MAN SPONGE AND BOY PATRICK!

The two friends bumped their fists together and approached Man Ray, who was still pretending to weep. SpongeBob cleared his throat to get his attention. "Um, Mr. Man Ray? We could teach you how to be good! And then we'll let you go!"

Man Ray stood up and looked grateful. "Ah, that would be fantastic!" he said. Then he turned away and spoke quietly to himself. "I'll fake my way through this just like I did in high school." He chuckled and rubbed his hands together gleefully.

SpongeBob and Patrick found a school desk in the depths of the Mermalair and invited Man Ray to sit in it. He sat down and politely folded his hands on top of the desk.

"Okay, Man Ray," SpongeBob said. "Are you ready for your first day at Goodness School?"

Man Ray quickly placed an apple on top of the desk. SpongeBob was impressed. *What a nice gift for a pupil to give his teacher!*

SpongeBob elbowed his sidekick. "Pat, get your wallet out." He turned back to Man Ray. "Okay, Goodness Lesson Number One: You see someone drop their wallet."

Patrick just stood there holding his wallet. SpongeBob whispered, "Patrick, drop the wallet." He dropped his wallet on the cave floor.

SpongeBob addressed Man Ray. "Now, what would you do?"

Man Ray got up from his desk, picked up the wallet, and politely offered it to Patrick. "Excuse me, sir, but I do believe you've dropped your wallet."

Patrick stared at the wallet. "It doesn't look familiar to me."

This answer took Man Ray by surprise. "What? I just saw you drop it." He offered the wallet again. "Here."

Patrick didn't take it. "Nope. It's not mine."

Man Ray tried to stay patient. "It is yours. I am trying to be a good person and return it to you."

"Return what to who?" Patrick said dully.

Man Ray slapped his hand to his face in frustration. Then he got an idea. He opened the wallet and found Patrick's ID card. "Aren't you Patrick Star?"

"Yup," Patrick said, nodding.

Man Ray showed the ID card to Patrick. "And this is your ID?"

"Yup," Patrick said.

Man Ray smiled. This was going well. "I found this ID in this wallet. And if that's the case, this must be your wallet!"

Patrick agreed. "That makes sense to me."

Man Ray put the ID back in the wallet and offered it to Patrick. "Then take it!"

"It's not my wallet," Patrick said.

Furious, Man Ray crushed the wallet in his hand and raised it above his head threateningly. "You dim bulb! Take back your wallet or I'll rip your arms off!" he roared.

Suddenly the Tickle Belt vibrated. Man Ray clutched his stomach and bent over, laughing.

"Wrong!" SpongeBob said sternly as he pushed the button on the belt's remote control.

"Good people don't rip other people's arms off!"

GOODNESS LESSON #2

SpongeBob stood ready to press the Tickle Belt button again if Man Ray turned violent. "Okay, Goodness Lesson Number Two," he said.

Patrick entered the cave room carrying a cardboard box. SpongeBob gestured toward him, asking Man Ray, "You see someone struggling with a heavy package. What do you do?"

As Patrick walked forward, huffing and puffing, Man Ray said, "Hello, friend! I noticed you were struggling with that package. Would you like some help with—"

WHAAM!!

Patrick accidentally dropped the heavy box on Man Ray's foot. "OW!" Man Ray yelled.

"Oops," Patrick said. "Sorry. Can I start over?"

He picked up the box. Man Ray reached for it, saying, "I noticed you were—"

SLAAM!!

Patrick accidently dropped the box on Man Ray's foot again! "OWWW!" Man Ray howled.

"Oops! Gotta start again," Patrick said, picking up the box.

"Would you—YAAAAAHHH!" Man Ray wailed. Patrick had dropped the box on his foot for the third time. "Oops," he said.

Man Ray pointed at Patrick, shaking with anger. "You butter-fingered pink thing! What's in that box, anyhow?"

"My wallets," Patrick answered.

"YAARRGGHHH!" Man Ray yelled. He grabbed the top of Patrick's head and lifted him off the ground.

"SpongeBob! Tickle him!" Patrick cried.

Man Ray slammed Patrick onto the cave floor. Then he lifted him up and did it again. And again!

SpongeBob punched the button, turning on the Tickle Belt. Man Ray started laughing but kept throwing Patrick around.

"It tickles!" Man Ray gasped between laughs. "But it's worth it!"

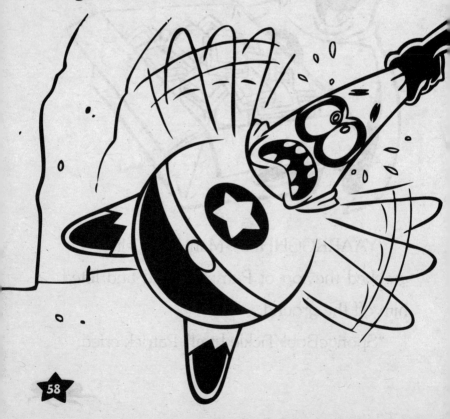

GOODNESS LESSON #3

SpongeBob stood holding the remote control. "All right, Goodness Lesson Number Three." He put his finger to his chin, thinking. "Uh, let's see . . ."

Patrick snatched the control from SpongeBob. He was wearing bandages and sitting in a wheelchair.

"I've got one," he said, scowling at Man Ray. "I'm

thinking of a number between one and one hundred. What is it?"

Man Ray looked confused. He scratched his head. "Um . . . sixty-two?"

"Wrong!" Patrick cried, punching the button on the remote control.

The belt started vibrating, tickling Man Ray. "HEE HEE HEE! STOP! STOP! HA HA HA!"

But Patrick kept pressing the button, tickling Man Ray more and more. SpongeBob looked concerned. "Hey, Patrick," he said. "That's got nothing to do with being good." He grabbed the remote control and tried to yank it away from Patrick.

"Let go of it, SpongeBob," Patrick snarled, still mad at Man Ray for hurting him.

"Pat, we've got to use it only when he's bad!" SpongeBob argued.

"Let go!" Patrick insisted.

"No, *you* let go!" SpongeBob said.

While they wrestled over the remote control, Man Ray was helplessly rolling on the floor, laughing and giggling.

"This is NOT the Man Sponge and Boy Patrick way!" SpongeBob yelled.

"Maybe not," Patrick said. "But it's the Patrick way!"

"LET . . . GO!" SpongeBob and Patrick said at the same time.

Then . . .

The remote control pulled apart, flew out of their hands, and broke into a thousand pieces. The belt started to tickle Man Ray even more deeply, and there was nothing SpongeBob could do to stop it!

"HA HA HA HA!" Man Ray laughed. "Frequency rising . . . belt out of control . . . belt on too high . . . tickling my DNA!"

Man Ray laughed until tears came out of his eyes. "Make it stop! PLEASE!"

SpongeBob and Patrick looked at each other, surprised.

GRADUATION DAY

As Man Ray kept laughing helplessly, SpongeBob turned to Patrick. "Did you hear that, Patrick?"

"Man Ray laughing?" Patrick asked. "I sure did. I wonder what's so funny."

SpongeBob shook his head. "No, I mean he said the *P*-word!"

"Peanuts?" Patrick guessed.

"Nope," SpongeBob said.

"Patrick?"

"Nope. Man Ray said 'please'!"

Patrick realized SpongeBob was right. He *had* said "please"!

"Well," Patrick said, shrugging, "that's good enough for me. I guess he's reconstituted."

"Rehabilitated," SpongeBob whispered to his friend, gently correcting him.

"Gesundheit," Patrick said.

SpongeBob pulled a big brass key out of his pocket and held it up in the air triumphantly. "It's Graduation Day, Man Ray!" he announced. "This is the key to your future!"

Man Ray was still writhing on the floor, laughing uncontrollably. SpongeBob started to walk over to him, but Patrick grabbed his arm, stopping him.

"Wait a minute, SpongeBob," he said. "Are you sure this is right?"

"What do you mean?" SpongeBob asked. "You said yourself he was reconstituted—I mean rehabilitated."

"I mean, if this is his Graduation Day, shouldn't there be music? And a diploma? And a guest speaker?" Patrick asked.

SpongeBob frowned, thinking. "We don't really have time for all that, Patrick. Besides, who would be the guest speaker?"

"Um, Man Sponge?" Patrick suggested. "Ooh! Ooh! Or, I know, Boy Patrick!"

Man Ray continued to squirm on the floor. His stomach was getting really sore from all the laughing.

"Well, Boy Patrick," SpongeBob said, "if you want to, feel free to provide the music."

"You got it, Man Sponge!" Patrick said. He started to sing a solemn song with no words. "Bum bum-bum-bum bum-bum, bum bum-bum-bum bum-bum . . ."

In time to the music SpongeBob marched over to Man Ray. He put the key in the belt's lock and turned it. The belt sprang open and stopped vibrating. Man Ray stopped laughing.

Then Man Ray smiled . . . an evil, devious smile. He leaped to his feet and raised both arms in triumph.

"Just look at him, Patrick," SpongeBob said happily. "The picture of goodness!"

Patrick put his arm around SpongeBob's shoulders, pleased with their excellent teaching.

Then Man Ray dashed over to the wall of superhero secret gadgetry!

THE SMELL OF DEFEAT

Chuckling with evil delight, Man Ray pulled a dangerous-looking gadget from the wall. It was a shiny metal glove that went all the way up to the wearer's elbow.

SpongeBob raised a finger to get Man Ray's attention. "Um, we're not supposed to touch that stuff."

But Man Ray just ignored SpongeBob, slipping the glove onto his left arm. With his right arm he clicked on the glove, getting it ready for action.

SpongeBob looked worried. "We're not supposed to touch that either."

Man Ray turned back to the wall again and reached for something that looked like an explosive hand grenade. Sniggering, he attached it to the metal glove.

"We're *really* not supposed to touch those, sir," SpongeBob pleaded, putting his hands up as if to say *stop*.

Laughing cruelly, Man Ray raised the index finger on the metal glove and aimed it right at SpongeBob and Patrick!

But SpongeBob just went right on lecturing Man Ray. "Good people have no use for weapons such as those . . ."

ZAAAP!

Man Ray fired a blast of energy right at SpongeBob and Patrick! They were lifted off the ground, their skeletons showing through their skin. "YAAAAGGGHHH!" they screamed.

Man Ray pointed his smoking finger in the air and scowled at his two victims. "The only thing I'm good at is being evil!" he snarled.

Then he turned and pressed a button on the wall. The door to the Mermalair slid open. As he ran out into Bikini Bottom, Man Ray called back over his shoulder, "So long, hopeless do-gooders!"

SpongeBob and Patrick were left behind. They were smoldering piles of ash and soot. They were also very disappointed in their Goodness student.

"What's that smell?" Patrick asked.

SpongeBob sighed. "That, Patrick, is the smell of defeat."

"Oh," Patrick said. "I thought it was my skin."

SpongeBob shrugged off his disappointment and raised his smoky chin. "Forget about your skin, Patrick! Man Ray is still bad and someone has to stop him!"

SpongeBob was full of determination. "This is a job for Man Sponge!"

"And Boy Patrick!" Patrick added.

TO THE RESCUE!

SpongeBob and Patrick scooted across the floor toward a pair of ropes that led to a lower level of the Mermalair. They leaped onto the ropes and slid down to the lower level. When they reached the bottom, they were dressed as superheroes! Man Sponge and Boy Patrick, that is!

"How are we going to catch up with Man Ray, Man Sponge?" the faithful sidekick asked. "He's pretty speedy."

"True, Boy Patrick, true." Man Sponge used all the power of his spongy brain. "I know! We'll

borrow the Invisible Boatmobile!"

"But wasn't that one of the things we weren't supposed to touch?" Boy Patrick pointed out.

That was a good point, so Man Sponge again put his brain to work. "Well," he said, "SpongeBob and Patrick weren't supposed to touch the Invisible Boatmobile. But they didn't say anything about Man Sponge and Boy Patrick!"

Boy Patrick brightened. "That is good thinking, SpongeBob!

I mean, Man Sponge!"

"Now all we have to do is find it!"

They started walking around the lower chamber of the Mermalair with their arms stretched out, hoping to feel the Invisible Boatmobile.

"Found it!" Boy Patrick shouted. "But it might need to be fixed. It's squishy and full of holes."

"Boy Patrick, that's not the Boatmobile. That's my head," Man Sponge said.

They kept feeling around until Man Sponge finally found the Invisible Boatmobile.

He climbed into the driver's seat, and Boy Patrick got in next to him.

"IGNITION ON!" Boy Patrick yelled, punching an invisible button on the dashboard. The engine roared.

"WAIT!" Man Sponge cried. "I don't have a license!"

Boy Patrick thought for a moment. Then he reached into his pocket.  "Well, this is an invisible boat, right?"

"Right . . . ," Man Sponge agreed.

"So you need an invisible license!" Boy Patrick concluded. He held up an invisible license and handed it to Man Sponge.

"You're the best sidekick ever, Boy Patrick!"

Man Sponge said, accepting the invisible license gratefully.

Man Sponge grasped the steering wheel and hit the gas. Flames burst out of the back of the Invisible Boatmobile and the boat shot forward.

SMASH!

The heroes crashed through the rock wall of the Mermalair!

"YAAAAAAAAAAAAGGGHHHH!" they screamed.

WHAM!

The Invisible Boatmobile slammed into a light pole. "Thank goodness for invisible seat belts," Boy Patrick said.

Man Ray ran right past them.

"Out of my way, fools!" he sneered. "You no longer have control of me."

He stopped on a rocky outcropping and pointed at Bikini Bottom. "Now this town belongs to Man Ray!"

"Not so fast, arch-villain!" Man Sponge said, climbing out of the boat. "We still have the Orb of Confusion. Take this!"

Man Sponge flipped the switch on the orb. Immediately he and Boy Patrick felt very confused. "Daaaahhh! Doy! Daa heyoooo!" they drooled.

Man Ray shrugged. "Well, that was easy." He left the two heroes babbling and headed straight for the First Nautical Bank!

GIVE ME YOUR HA HA HAS

At the bank several customers stood in line waiting for their turns with the teller. "You know what I like about this bank?" one lady asked another. "It's always so nice and quiet." The other customers nodded in agreement.

Just then . . .

BOOM!

Man Ray kicked open the bank's front door and leaped inside. "All right, people!" he roared. "Everybody stand right where you are!" He pointed the index finger of his metal glove right at the customers, ready to fire.

The customers gasped. It looked as though the bank was being robbed!

Seeing the customers cower, Man Ray smiled to himself. He had them right where he wanted them. Now all he had to do was take their cash and all the money in the bank.

"I want all of you to . . . ," he said, starting to give them instructions.

HA!

But suddenly, he felt the strangest urge to laugh!

"I . . . heh heh . . . want you to . . . hee hee hee," he giggled.

Unable to stop himself, Man Ray let out a big laugh. "Ha ha ha!"

HA!

The customers were puzzled. What was going on? Was this guy trying to rob the bank or was this some kind of joke?

The teller snickered. The customers started to giggle too.

"No! No!" Man Ray shouted. He was losing control of the situation! "Stop giggling or I'll have to . . . haw haw haw!"

"Ha ha ha!" the customers laughed, thinking the whole thing must be a prank. "Ho ho hee hee hee!"

"STOP LAUGHING, YOU FOOLS!"

Man Ray bellowed. He shoved his way past the customers and went right up to the teller.

"What can I do for you, sir?" she asked politely.

Man Ray pointed his metal glove right in her face. "I'll tell you what you can do!" he yelled angrily. "Give me all your . . . heh heh heh!"

The teller looked bewildered. "All my what, sir?"

Man Ray struggled to stop laughing. "Give me all your . . . hee hee hee!" He clutched his ribs, hooting and snorting.

"I'm sorry, sir, but I still don't understand what it is that you want me to do," the teller said patiently.

Summoning all his strength, Man Ray tried to stop laughing. "GIVE ME . . . ," he started to say, but it was no use. "HAW HAW HAW HAW HAW!"

He pounded the counter, laughing. He fell to the ground and kicked his heels, rolling around and hugging his sides. He'd never laughed so hard in his life!

Finally he sat up. "The belt is gone," he

said, "but I still feel its tickle!" Then he realized
he didn't feel evil anymore. "The urge to do
bad is gone," he said, amazed.

Man Ray fell to his knees, defeated. "I
guess I'll just open a checking account," he
said.

GOODNESS RULES

Back outside the Mermalair, Man Sponge and Boy Patrick were still caught in the befuddling rays coming from the Orb of Confusion.

"DOOOOYYYY!" Man Sponge said with his tongue hanging out of his mouth.

"DUUUUHHHH!" Boy Patrick said with his eyes crossed.

Man Ray calmly walked up and switched off the orb.

"DOYEEEE . . . ," Man Sponge said. Then the confusion left him. He looked up and saw the arch-villain he'd been trying to stop!

"Man Ray!" he gasped.

Man Ray held up a friendly hand in a gesture of peace. "No need to be alarmed, SpongeBob," he said.

"That's Man Sponge," he corrected.

"Whatever," Man Ray said. "Your teachings have transformed me!"

Man Sponge was astonished. "You mean, you aren't evil anymore?"

Man Ray shook his head. "Nope. You tickled the evil right out of me." Then he held up his new checkbook and smiled. "And," he added, "I have checks with little poodles on them!"

Man Sponge leaned forward to look at the checks. Sure enough, they featured pictures of adorable little poodles!

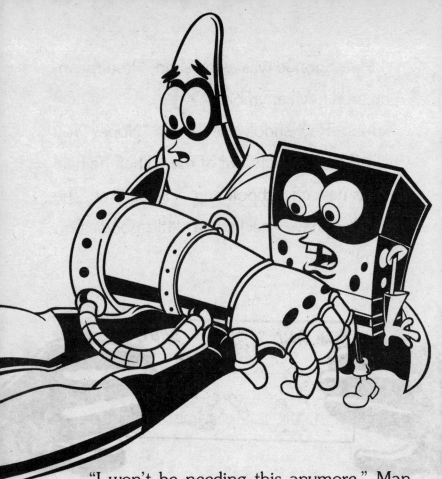

"I won't be needing this anymore," Man
Ray said, taking off the metal glove he'd
stolen from the Mermalair. He handed it to
Man Sponge.

"Thanks," SpongeBob said, staggering a
little under the weight of the heavy glove.

Man Ray smiled. Then he turned and strolled away. As he went, he waved back over his shoulder. "Farewell, fellow do-gooders!"

"Bye, Man Ray!" Man Sponge called, waving. He turned to his sidekick. "Wow, Boy Patrick! We did it! We saved the day!"

"We did?" Boy Patrick asked.

"We sure did! We took an evil arch-villain and we turned him good! He'll never bother anyone in Bikini Bottom again!" Man Sponge cheered.

"Wow," Boy Patrick said. "It's like we're superheroes or something."

Man Sponge nodded. "That's because we ARE superheroes! We're Man Sponge . . ."

"And Boy Patrick!"

They pumped their fists and jumped in the air. What a triumph! What an achievement! What an accomplishment!

Mermaidman and Barnacleboy themselves couldn't have done it better.

THE END

WHAT WERE YOU SHRINKING?

By David Lewman

SPONGE PATROL

It was a quiet day in Bikini Bottom, and SpongeBob and Patrick were eager for an adventure.

"I think it's time, Patrick," SpongeBob told his best friend seriously.

"Time for what?" Patrick asked.

"For some superhero action!" SpongeBob cried out.

Five seconds later, Man Sponge and Boy Patrick marched through downtown Bikini Bottom on their daily rounds. The two superheroes were eager to help anyone in trouble.

"Keep a sharp eye out for citizens in need," Man Sponge reminded Boy Patrick.

"Aye-aye, Man Sponge," Boy Patrick answered, saluting.

Suddenly, Man Sponge pointed. "Look, Boy Patrick! A person in distress!"

Boy Patrick peered in the direction Man Sponge was pointing. "You mean that trash can? You're right! It needs to be emptied!"

"No, I mean the lady next to the trash can!" Man Sponge explained. "She obviously wants to cross the street, but she can't get through the villainous traffic without the aid of . . . MAN SPONGE AND . . ."

"BOY PATRICK!" added Boy Patrick. Together they rushed over to the elderly woman, picked her up, and dashed across the street!

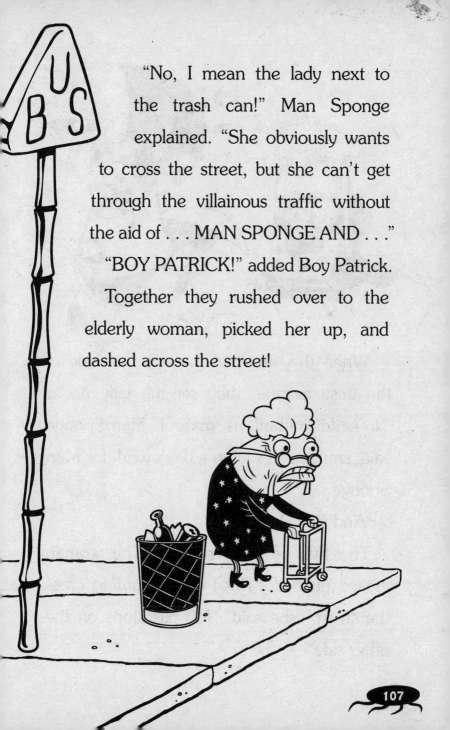

When they reached the opposite side of the busy avenue, they set the lady down. "No need to thank us, ma'am!" Man Sponge said, smiling. "It's all in a day's work for Man Sponge . . ."

"And Boy Patrick!"

The two of them ran off. The woman looked puzzled. "But I didn't *want* to cross the street," she said. "My bus stops on the other side."

By that time, Man Sponge had already moved on to another citizen in need. "Boy Patrick, if I'm not mistaken—and I never am—that young fellow there is being attacked by a vicious creature!"

Without a second's hesitation, the two superheroes sprinted over and got between the beast and the boy. "Run, lad!" shouted

109

Man Sponge. "We'll handle the monster!"

The boy looked confused. "What monster?"

Man Sponge pointed at the fearsome beast. "That monster right there!"

The boy looked insulted. "That's not a monster! That's my pet worm, Crawler. I'm taking him for a walk. Come on, boy."

The worm happily followed its owner. Boy Patrick looked concerned. "I don't like this,

Man Sponge. It's like that monster has the kid under some kind of mind-control ray!"

"There's no time to think about that!" Man Sponge cried. "We've got to save Pearl from the evil Teenage Guy!"

Sure enough, right across the street was Mr. Krabs's daughter, Pearl. She was chatting with a teenage boy.

"Um, Pearl," he asked nervously. "Do you think maybe you might like to, um, go with me to the, um, dance next—"

"HOLD IT RIGHT THERE, TEENAGE GUY!" Man Sponge bellowed. "That fair, young damsel is under the constant protection of Man Sponge . . ."

"And Boy Patrick!" chimed in Boy Patrick.

Pearl looked annoyed. Derek had finally gotten up the nerve to ask her to the dance, and then these two come barging in! "Shouldn't you be at work?" she snapped.

Man Sponge looked at his watch and gasped. "Gadzooks!" he cried. "The lass is right! I'm due at the Krusty Krab, where I toil under the guise of my mild-mannered secret identity, SpongeBob SquarePants!" He dashed off to work.

Derek watched him go. "You know, it's not much of a secret identity if you announce it to everyone," he said.

He and Pearl stood there awkwardly with Patrick for a minute. "So," Patrick asked, "you two want to get a milk shake?"

KRABBY HEROES

SpongeBob zipped through the dining room of the Krusty Krab. "Hi, Squidward! It's just me, SpongeBob, ready for work!"

"What a surprise," Squidward said dryly. SpongeBob hurried into the kitchen and got to work cooking Krabby Patties. The only thing he loved more than patrolling Bikini Bottom as Man Sponge was his wonderful job at the Krusty Krab.

Out front, Mermaidman burst into the dining room. "Through the double doors, away!" he cried.

His faithful sidekick, Barnacleboy, followed him into the restaurant. "I told you," he said. "I'm not hungry, Mermaidman."

Shocked, Mermaidman whipped around to face his loyal assistant. "Nonsense, Barnacleboy!" he insisted. "We've got to keep up our strength for the fight against . . . **EEEEEEEVVVIIIIIIL!"**

Barnacleboy looked around the fast-food restaurant. "What a dive," he muttered.

"To the register, away!" Mermaidman announced as he ran toward Squidward to place his order.

"Can I help you?" asked Squidward, sounding as if the last thing he wanted to do was help anyone.

Mermaidman studied the menu hanging on the wall above Squidward's head. "A double Krabby Patty and Coral Bits for me," he said. "And a Silly Meal for the lad," he added, pointing his thumb toward Barnacleboy.

"It's not for the toy!" Barnacleboy explained, feeling a little embarrassed. "I just gotta fit in the tights." Squidward could not have cared less. "Whatever," he said. "Five dollars, please."

"You got it, Bucky!" Mermaidman said. He rummaged around in his coin purse and pulled out a button. "Will this cover it?"

"No," Squidward said, looking disgusted.

Barnacleboy leaned in close to Squidward. "Listen, big nose," he said, glaring. "That guy's been saving your butt since before you were born. Don't you have a living-legend discount or something?"

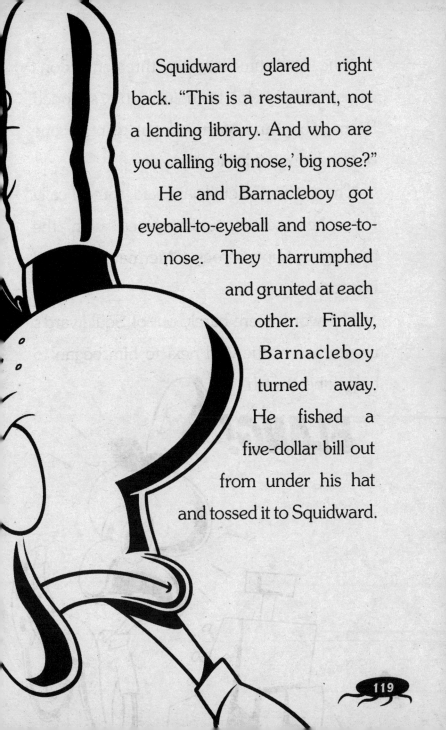

Squidward glared right back. "This is a restaurant, not a lending library. And who are you calling 'big nose,' big nose?"

He and Barnacleboy got eyeball-to-eyeball and nose-to-nose. They harrumphed and grunted at each other. Finally, Barnacleboy turned away. He fished a five-dollar bill out from under his hat and tossed it to Squidward.

"The next time danger threatens, don't expect any help from us!" he snapped. Barnacleboy and Mermaidman went to one of the dining tables to sit down.

"I'm shaking," Squidward said, sarcastically. Then he snorted, unimpressed with the two aging superheroes. "Mermaidman and Barnacleboy—"

The words were barely out of Squidward's mouth before the wall next to him began to bulge and stretch.

BLANG!

SpongeBob burst through the wall into the
dining area.

"MERMAIDMAN AND BARNACLEBOY!"
he said loudly, his voice trembling
with excitement. "MUST . . . GET . . .
AUTOGRAPH!"

FINDERS KEEPERS

Without a moment to lose, SpongeBob sprang into action. He shot his right arm across the room and grabbed a pen from a customer's pocket. He stretched his left arm out a window and snatched a piece of paper floating by. Now he was ready!

At their table, Mermaidman and Barnacleboy waited for their food. "If you want to grow up strong

like me," Mermaidman said, smiling, "you've gotta make room for seconds." He unfastened his belt, and his stomach popped out.

"Here comes our waiter!" he added.

But it was no waiter. It was SpongeBob, running toward their table, vibrating with anticipation.

"AUTOOGRAAAPH!"

he cried.

Barnacleboy looked alarmed. "Holy sea cow! It's that sponge kid!"

"Quick, lad!" Mermaidman said. "To the Invisible Boatmobile! Awaaay!"

Mermaidman leaped up. His pants fell down, revealing his polka-dot boxer shorts. He pulled them up and ran out of the Krusty Krab, followed by Barnacleboy.

Once outside, they stared at the crowded parking lot. "Where'd we park?" Barnacleboy asked.

"Uhhh . . . ," Mermaidman said, trying hard to remember.

Back inside the Krusty Krab, SpongeBob reached their table, overwhelmed.

"Can I have your autograph? Can I have your autograph?" he chattered. Then he realized his two favorite superheroes weren't there. "They're gone!"

Looking around to see where they went, SpongeBob spotted something on the floor and gasped. "Mermaidman's belt!"

Outside, Mermaidman and Barnacleboy were still searching for their boat. Then Mermaidman got an idea. "We'll find it with the Invisible Boat Alarm!"

He pulled an invisible remote control out of his pocket and pressed a button.

CHIRP, CHIRP!

CHIRP, CHIRP!

In a nearby parking place, the Invisible Boatmobile flashed into view, becoming visible for just a second.

Mermaidman pointed gleefully. "There she is!" He and Barnacleboy jumped, flying through the air, toward the Invisible Boatmobile.

Unfortunately, Barnacleboy landed right on the stick shift.

"YEOWWWCH!"

he cried.

"I told you we should have gotten the automatic!"

SpongeBob burst out of the Krusty Krab's front doors carrying Mermaidman's belt. "Hey, guys! Wait up! I've got something for you!"

But all Mermaidman and Barnacleboy saw was an overeager fan trying to get an autograph.

"Floor it!" Barnacleboy yelled.

Mermaidman hit the gas, and the invisible engine roared to life. Flames shot out the back of the boat, and the two superheroes sped off into the distance.

"You forgot your belt!" SpongeBob called.

But it was no use. The superheroes were gone.

ZAP!

PART I

SpongeBob looked at the belt and his eyes got big with wonder.

"Mermaidman's secret utility belt!" he said. "The emblem of submersible justice. For sixty-five years this belt has helped prevent the fall of nations. And pants. I can't believe I'm actually holding it in my hands."

SpongeBob started thinking about all the amazing Mermaidman and Barnacleboy adventures that featured the secret utility belt. There was one in particular that he remembered well. . . .

Mermaidman and Barnacleboy were surrounded by bad guys—the Dirty Bubble, Man Ray, Jumbo Shrimp, the Atomic Flounder. . . .

"We're in a pickle this time, Barnacleboy!" cried Mermaidman.

"Yep, we're in a jam for sure," agreed Barnacleboy.

Then a voice rang out. "Pickles taste terrible with jam!"

133

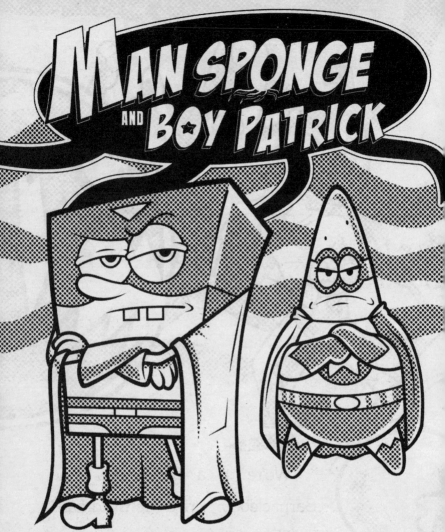

MAN SPONGE
AND BOY PATRICK

It was Man Sponge! And his faithful sidekick, Boy Patrick! They had arrived to help Mermaidman and Barnacleboy defeat the villains!

134

"Thank Neptune you're here, Man Sponge!" gushed Mermaidman. "These criminals have us outnumbered. And it's almost time for lunch."

"Stop stalling!" growled the Dirty Bubble. "Surrender or fight. It's up to you."

"But hurry," Man Ray snarled. "It's almost time for lunch."

"I just said that," Mermaidman protested. Then he turned to Man Sponge and whispered, "How do you think we should handle these ruffians? Got any brilliant ideas?"

"Brilliant ideas are the only kind Man Sponge has!" Boy Patrick said enthusiastically.

Man Sponge smiled. "Thanks, Boy Patrick." Then he concentrated, using all the power of his tremendous brain. "Well," he said to Mermaidman, "you could use your utility belt."

"Excellent plan!" Mermaidman cried. He looked down at his belt. "Let's see. Which ray should I use? The Heat Ray? The Cold Ray? The Tanning Ray?"

"I don't think tanning the bad guys is going to help," Barnacleboy said.

"How about the Blast Ray?" Man Sponge suggested.

"And quickly!" Boy Patrick added. The villains were closing in.

"You got it, Bucky!" Mermaidman said. He pressed a button on his belt.

WHAM!

A shock wave blasted out around the heroes. It left the good guys unharmed, but knocked the bad guys far, far away.

"That's the ticket!" Barnacleboy shouted, clapping his hands with glee.

"Thank you, Man Sponge!" Mermaidman said, shaking his hand. "We couldn't have done it without you! If anyone deserves to borrow this belt anytime they want, it's you!"

At least, that's the way I remember it, SpongeBob thought as his mind returned to the present. "Well, I guess I should return the belt."

He started to walk in the direction Mermaidman and Barnacleboy had driven. Suddenly, he had a change of heart. He turned on his heel and sprinted back to the Krusty Krab!

Wearing the belt, he slammed the kitchen door and leaned up against it. "Or maybe not!" he said, giggling mischievously.

"I could just hold on to it until after work," he said, talking himself into it.

SpongeBob looked down at the belt fastened around his square pants. "All alone with Mermaidman's belt. . . . I wonder what this button does?"

WHALE OF A TALE

A beam of strange light came out of the belt. It hit a barrel of pickles. The barrel shrank, pickles and all, until it was as tiny as a thimble!

SpongeBob balanced the barrel of pickles on the end of his finger. "Wow," he marveled. "The Small Ray!"

He remembered one time when Mermaidman had used the Small Ray. . . .

Man Sponge and Boy Patrick were finishing up another day of keeping Bikini Bottom safe when Mermaidman and Barnacleboy drove up in the Invisible Boatmobile.

"Man Sponge! Come quickly! There's a new villain in town and we need your help!" Mermaidman said.

Man Sponge and Boy Patrick hopped in the backseat. They roared off, heading toward City Hall.

When they got there, they ran into the mayor's office. The mayor had been tied up. Sitting in his chair was the biggest fish that Man Sponge had ever seen!

Mermaidman pointed an accusing finger at the huge fish. "Get out of the mayor's chair immediately!" he ordered.

The gigantic fish chuckled a low, menacing laugh. Then he stood up. His head grazed the ceiling. "You listen to me, pal. I'm Whale Shark, and I'm the biggest fish in the sea! That means, what I say goes."

"Not if I have anything to say about it!"

Mermaidman said bravely.

Whale Shark took one step and loomed over Mermaidman. "Oh, yeah?" he asked. "And what exactly do you have to say about it, little man?"

Mermaidman gulped. "Well, I haven't exactly had time to put my thoughts in order. I'm really better with a prepared speech. . . ."

Things looked bad for Mermaidman

and Barnacleboy. Just as Whale Shark was about to attack them, Man Sponge shouted, "Mermaidman! Your belt! THE SMALL RAY!"

"Oh, yeah!" Mermaidman cried. He punched a button on his belt.

ZZZAAAAAAP!!

The strange beam hit Whale Shark, making him glow for a second. Then he shrank down to the size of a sea nut! "Hey!" he squeaked. "What'd you do to me?!"

"Yay!" Boy Patrick cheered, picking up Whale Shark with no problem.

Mermaidman turned to Man Sponge. "Thanks, Man Sponge! We couldn't have done it without you!"

Man Sponge blushed modestly. "Oh, it was nothing, really. . . ."

At least, that was the way SpongeBob remembered it.

He couldn't resist playing with the Small Ray, and soon he had created a tiny Krusty Krab kitchen with things that he'd shrunk!

Squidward heard all the zapping and laughing and came into the kitchen to investigate. "SpongeBob, what's going on in here?" he asked.

Squidward stared at all the things SpongeBob had shrunk. His hat, his spatula—even a miniature Krabby Patty for a bug to eat at a little table!

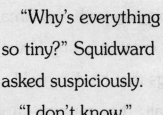

"Why's everything
so tiny?" Squidward
asked suspiciously.

"I don't know,"
SpongeBob replied
sheepishly, trying to
hide the belt behind his
back.

"What have you got there?"
Squidward asked.

"Nothing!"

"No really,
let's see it!"
Then he gasped.
"Is that Mermaidman's
belt?!"

"Yes." SpongeBob's
teeth chattered with
nerves.

"Wow, I find it hard to believe he'd lend it to you!" Squidward remarked.

"Me . . . either . . . hee, hee," SpongeBob let out.

Squidward gasped with disbelief when the truth finally sank in. "He didn't lend it to you . . . did he?"

SQUIDWARD'S REVENGE

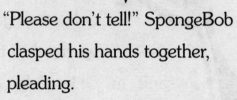

"Please don't tell!" SpongeBob clasped his hands together, pleading.

Squidward pointed at SpongeBob accusingly. "You STOLE it!"

"PLEASE DON'T TELL!"

SpongeBob begged.

"Oh, I'm telling," Squidward said, nodding. This was the perfect opportunity to get back at SpongeBob for driving him crazy every day at work.

"Squidward," SpongeBob said desperately.
"If Mermaidman finds out, he'll kick me out of
his fan club for sure. Please don't tell!"

Squidward pointed his thumb over his
shoulder at the phone hanging on the kitchen
wall. "Uh-oh," he said.
"There's the phone!"

SpongeBob clutched
his head frantically. "NO!"
Squidward started
backing toward the wall.

"I'm walking toward the phone. . . ."

"NO!!!" SpongeBob screamed, reaching out toward Squidward.

"I'm getting closer to the phone," Squidward said. He thoroughly enjoyed toying with SpongeBob. He stretched one tentacle toward the phone. . . .

"NOOOO!" SpongeBob sobbed.

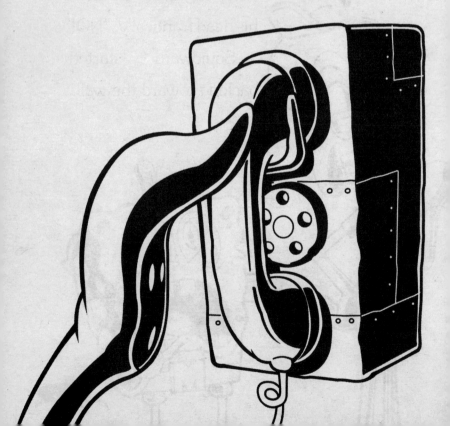

Squidward picked up the phone. "And now,
the moment we've all been waiting for . . ."

"I'M BEGGING YOU!" SpongeBob cried.

"Hello, I'd like to speak to Mermaidma—"

ZZZZAAAP!

ZAP! PART II

Squidward dropped the phone's receiver as he flew up in the air and landed on a chopping block next to a knife and a tomato. He was tiny! "What did you do to me?!" he cried.

The phone bonked Squidward on the head as it fell down. He could hear Mermaidman saying, "Hello? Hello?"

SpongeBob hung up the phone and said sadly, "I'm sorry, Squidward, but you made me do it."

Squidward pointed his tentacle at SpongeBob angrily. "SpongeBob, if you don't return me to normal size RIGHT NOW, you are gonna be in really big trouble!"

SpongeBob grasped Mermaidman's belt nervously. "Uh, okay. Uh . . ." He had no idea how to unshrink Squidward!

"I said now!" Squidward yelled.

"Uh . . . ," SpongeBob said, staring down at the controls on the belt. There were buttons of all shapes, colors, and sizes. There were complicated switches and dials . . . and he had no idea what any of them did!

"DO YOU HEAR ME?!" Squidward shouted as loud as he could.

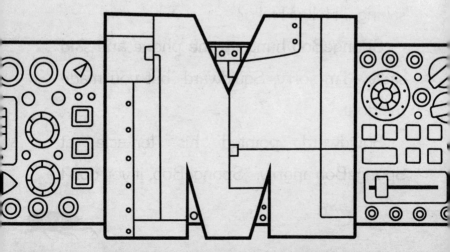

Holding his breath, SpongeBob pushed a button. He hoped it would return Squidward to his normal size.

ZZZZAAAAAPP!!

"YAAHHH!" Squidward shrieked. He looked like he had a hundred eyes, and there were tiny snakes growing out of his head!

"Holy fish paste! Get it off me!" he screeched. "Get it off me!" Squidward grabbed the clump of eyes and snakes and tossed it away.

He was breathing hard. "Don't you know how to work that thing?" he gasped.

SpongeBob tried to look confident. "Uh, I can do it," he claimed uncertainly. He picked another button and pressed it.

ZAP!

Squidward's nose grew until it was the size of his whole body!

ZAAAAP!

His nose shrank, but now his feet were huge!

ZZAP!

His feet shrank, but now he was freezing cold!

ZAPP!

Now he was burning hot!

ZAAP!

Now he started whirling around like a tornado!

ZZZAAAAAPP!!

Now he couldn't stop dancing wildly!

ZZZZAAP!

Now he looked
like he was made
out of mud!

ZAPP!!

Now he looked like he was made out of stone!

ZAAAP!

Squidward stood on the chopping block with smoke rising from his skin. He was still tiny!

"STOP!" he screamed. All these changes were extremely uncomfortable, and none of them were getting Squidward back to his normal size.

"I've got an idea!" Squidward said. "Let's call Mermaidman and—"

"NO!" SpongeBob cried. He grabbed Squidward and picked him up. "I can't let you do that!"

SpongeBob thought hard. What should he do? He couldn't leave Squidward tiny, but he couldn't get kicked out of Mermaidman's fan club.

"There must be someone else who can help," he said. "Someone smart and wise with years of life experience . . ."

OH, PICKLE!

Patrick was leaning on his rock house, waiting for SpongeBob to come home from the Krusty Krab. He was looking forward to being Boy Patrick again.

SpongeBob ran up, waving his hands. "Patrick! Patrick!" he called frantically.

"Man Sponge!" Patrick answered. "Boy Patrick is ready for action!"

But SpongeBob didn't have time to *play* superhero. He had a *real* superhero problem to solve! The words tumbled out as he nervously explained, "Patrick, I was at work, and Mermaidman and Barnacleboy came, and then I got this belt, and look!"

He reached in his pocket and pulled out Squidward, who was still very, very small. He held him up for Patrick to see.

Patrick was excited. "A Squidward action figure!" he gasped. "Let me play with him!"

Before SpongeBob could explain that the little figure was the *real* Squidward, Patrick snatched him out of SpongeBob's hand. "Fighter pilot!" he exclaimed, delighted with the new "toy."

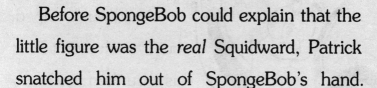

He moved Squidward around, back and forth, up and down, as though he were zooming through the air in a jet. "Dive bomb!" Patrick shouted.

Squidward yelped, but Patrick didn't hear his shrunken voice.

"Let's see how far I can throw it!" Patrick dared.

"Patrick, no!" SpongeBob yelled, putting out his hands to stop him. "That's not an action figure! That's the real Squidward. I shrank him by accident."

"Ohhh," Patrick said, holding Squidward still. Then he cocked his arm, ready to toss a forward pass. "Let's see how far I can throw him!"

Squidward screamed. SpongeBob stopped Patrick again.

"Wait! You don't

understand! This is serious. I don't know how to unshrink him. He could be stuck like this for the rest of his life."

SpongeBob looked really worried. Patrick tried to reassure him.

"Aw, don't worry about it," Patrick said. "He'll find love one day."

"You think so?" SpongeBob asked.

"Sure!" Patrick said confidently. "But it'll be with someone his own size. Like this pickle!"

Patrick held up a pickle. Sure enough, it was just about the same size as shrunken Squidward.

"See?" Patrick said happily. "They like each other!"

Squidward frowned at the pickle. Patrick started to move the pickle toward Squidward. "No, no, no, no . . . !" he said.

But Patrick couldn't hear Squidward's tiny voice. He pushed the pickle right

into Squidward's face, making kissing sounds. "Mwah! Mwah! Mwah!"

"Bleah!" Squidward grunted.

SpongeBob sighed and looked down at Mermaidman's belt. "If only I knew how to work this thing," he said.

Patrick got excited. "You know what?" he asked. "This is just like one of my favorite episodes of *The Adventures of Mermaidman and Barnacleboy*! And lucky for you," Patrick said proudly, "I remember exactly how it went!"

WUMBORAMA

"Mermaidman was talking to his friend, Barnacleguy—" Patrick said.

"Barnacleboy," SpongeBob corrected.

Patrick struck a very dramatic pose. "Mermaidman screamed, 'I sense WEEVILS!'"

"I think you mean 'evil,'" SpongeBob said.

Patrick broke out of his pose. "Who's telling this story? You or me?"

"Sorry," SpongeBob said.

"So Mermaidman and Barnacleboy ran to Boy Patrick for help," Patrick continued. "They needed him to help fight the scary weevils."

SpongeBob didn't remember this episode at all.

"Boy Patrick said, 'Don't worry! I will help you! I'm not afraid of ANYTHING!' So they jumped into the Inedible Boatmobile. . . ."

SpongeBob started to say something, but Patrick waved him off and kept telling his story.

"And drove to downtown Bikini Bottom, where the giant weevils were eating the buildings and then burping. And the burps smelled horrible. Like this."

Patrick gave a tremendous belch. Squidward looked sick.

"So Mermaidguy and Barnacledude turned

to Boy Patrick and screamed, 'Boy Patrick! What should we do?!'"

Patrick jumped up and down and waved his arms, acting out the story.

"And Boy Patrick thought really hard and then he said, 'Why don't you use your secret utility belt?' And so they did, and it worked, and Boy Patrick was a hero. The end."

At least that was the way Patrick remembered it. He crossed his arms and looked smug.

SpongeBob was puzzled. "That's a great story, Patrick. But what does it have to do with getting Squidward back to his normal size?"

"It proves," Patrick said patiently, "that I know all about Mermaidman's belt. Here, let me take a closer look."

Patrick leaned down and stared at the belt for

about a second. "Hmmm," he said, rubbing his chin. "You know what the problem is?"

"What?" asked SpongeBob eagerly.

"You've got it set on *M* for 'mini' when it should be set on *W* for 'wumbo'!" Patrick announced triumphantly. He grabbed the *M* belt buckle and turned it upside down so it looked like a *W*.

SpongeBob frowned. "Patrick, I don't think 'wumbo' is a real word."

Patrick just shook his head.

"Come on! You know, I wumbo; you wumbo; he, she, me wumbo. . . ."

Patrick still tightly clutched Squidward. He rolled his eyes as Patrick kept explaining.

"Wumboing, will have be wumbo? Wumborama? Wumbology, the study of wumbo? This is stuff you learn in first grade, SpongeBob!"

SpongeBob smiled. "Patrick, I'm sorry I doubted you."

"All right then," Patrick said. "Let her rip!"

ZZZZZAAAAAP!!

ZAP!

PART III

Patrick looked at Squidward. They were both the same size! "Yay!" Patrick cheered. "It worked!"

"Oh no!" SpongeBob cried. He reached down and picked up Patrick *and* Squidward.

Patrick pointed at SpongeBob. "Look! SpongeBob's giant! Can I be giant next?"

"Patrick, I'm not giant," SpongeBob explained. "You've shrunk too!"

Patrick was the same size as Squidward because the Small Ray had shrunk him! Now SpongeBob had *two* shrunken friends to worry about!

"You're kidding!" Patrick said, surprised. He reached in his pocket and pulled out the pickle he'd shoved into Squidward's face. "Good thing I've still got this pickle."

Patrick started kissing the pickle. "Mwah! Mwah! Mmmmwah!"

"HEY!" Squidward yelled to get SpongeBob's attention. "NOW will you take us to Mermaidman?"

SpongeBob looked horrified. "NO!" he yelped. "He must never find out!"

Squidward reeled back from being yelled at by someone so much bigger than him.

SpongeBob looked sorry. "But I'll think of something," he said. "I promise!"

He pulled a jar out of his pocket. "Until then, you'll be safe in this jar." He dropped Squidward and Patrick into the jar.

Patrick turned to Squidward. "You know what's funny? My pickle started out in a jar, and now it's in one again!" He shrugged. "Huh. It's like a pun or something." Patrick laughed, but Squidward was not amused.

SpongeBob was sweating nervously. He tried to reassure himself. "It's only two people. No big deal. Nobody saw it."

Just then Sandy walked up, startling SpongeBob.

"Howdy, SpongeBob!"

ZZAAAAABBBP!

Without even thinking, SpongeBob had whirled around and zapped Sandy with the Small Ray! Now she was tiny too!

"What did y'all do to me?" she asked, astonished to be so small.

"I'm sorry, Sandy!" SpongeBob cried. He tried to explain the whole mess as he put Sandy in his jar too. "You see,

Mermaidman came into the Krusty Krab and—"

Just then Larry the Lobster walked up behind SpongeBob, startling him again.

"Hey, SpongeBob!" Larry said.

SpongeBob screamed and caught the shrunken lobster in his jar.

Then another fish walked up and greeted SpongeBob.

ZZAAAPPP!

Then a girl fish.

ZZAAAAPPPP!!!...

Then Mrs. Puff.

ZZAAAAPPPP!!!...

Then Scooter,
the surfer fish.

189

ZZAAAAAAAPPPP!!!

Everywhere he went, SpongeBob bumped into more people who knew him. They all got shrunk and caught in the jar!

Soon he'd walked all the way downtown. He squeezed the lid onto his jar. "I'm going to have to get a bigger jar," he said.

SpongeBob looked around the deserted streets. He was all alone. He'd shrunk everyone in Bikini Bottom!

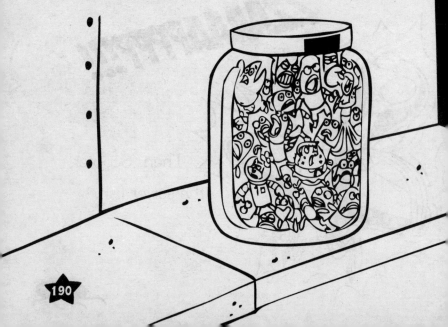

191

FISH JAR

Inside the jar, Squidward was pressed up against so many people. "SpongeBob, will you just face the facts?" he snarled. "You've got to go to Mermaidman!"

"Oh, Squidward," SpongeBob said, starting to sniffle. "He'll be so disappointed."

From inside the jar, Sandy snapped, "Well, you can't leave us small forever!"

SpongeBob fell to his knees and sobbed. "You don't understand!" he wailed.

But then a comforting voice said, "SpongeBob, you need to admit your mistake."

SpongeBob looked closely at the jar to see who had spoken. "Mom?" he asked as he wiped tears away from his eyes.

Then another voice spoke from inside the jar. "Your mother's right, son. Mermaidman will understand."

Barnacleboy turned to the speaker. "*You're* Mermaidman, you old coot!"

"Ohh, yeah," Mermaidman said.

He'd been shrunk and placed in the jar too!

SpongeBob turned the jar until he found his favorite superhero. "Mermaidman?" he said. "I'm so sorry! It's just that I'm such a big fan. And your belt—"

"Aw, don't worry, son," Mermaidman said reassuringly. "I understand. Why, I remember back when I first used the belt. The year was nineteen aught eleven-twelve. I believe the president then was—"

"JUST TELL HIM HOW TO UNSHRINK US!" everyone else in the jar shouted.

"Oh, uh, yes, the Unshrink Ray!" Mermaidman said, thinking hard. "Let's see, uh, um . . . did you set it to wumbo?"

The jarful of angry citizens couldn't believe their ears. "WHAT?!" they roared.

SpongeBob was holding the packed jar in his hands. It started to vibrate, then shake violently. He could barely hold on to it!

Then . . .

WHOOOOOOOOOSH!

It was too packed to hold everyone, and all of the shrunken people of Bikini Bottom came shooting out of the jar like a geyser! They flew up into the air and landed on the ground near SpongeBob.

The mob of tiny sea-dwellers formed themselves into words that made up a sentence. SpongeBob read the sentence out loud. . . .

TINY TOWN

The furious Bikini Bottomites rushed toward SpongeBob's shoes and climbed up his legs and started kicking!

Squidward quickly found his way up to SpongeBob's stomach. "Now I have to drive five miles to go to the bathroom . . . in my own home!"

He kicked SpongeBob's stomach.

OOOOOFF!

Sandy made it up to SpongeBob's head. "I need an elevator to climb one stair! HI-YAAH!" She gave his head a sharp karate chop.

YOUCH!

Mermaidman and Barnacleboy stood on SpongeBob's arms. Mermaidman said, "We've been shrinking for years . . ."

"But this is ridiculous!" Barnacleboy added. Caught up in the anger of the mob, they kicked SpongeBob too.

YEECH!

Angry fish were attacking every part of SpongeBob's giant body. He was knocked into every possible shape and weird position.

He clutched his head and saw stars. Then he heard the crowd shout something. . . .

"EVERYTHING'S TOO BIG!"

Suddenly, that gave SpongeBob an idea! He raised his index finger and said, "I've got it!"

From inside SpongeBob, Squidward and the others heard a familiar

ZZZZZZAAAAPP!!

Then they heard SpongeBob say, "Ta-da!"

They were eager to see what he'd shrunk this time and amazed when they realized that he hadn't shrunk *anyone*—he'd shrunk all the buildings in Bikini Bottom!

"Since I couldn't make you big," he explained, "I made the city small!"

The citizens poured out onto the streets to inspect their newly shrunken town.

"And now, only one more thing to shrink," SpongeBob said, lifting the buckle off Mermaidman's belt. He pointed it at himself like a camera. "Cheese!"

ZAP!

SpongeBob shrank down to everyone else's size.

Squidward looked around. "I guess this is okay," he said.

"Yeah!" Larry the Lobster agreed. "What's the difference?"

"Good job, SpongeBob!" another fish said. They all cheered!

"Another brilliant idea, Man Sponge!" Patrick shook SpongeBob's hand.

"Thanks, Boy Patrick!" SpongeBob said, grinning.

As everyone celebrated SpongeBob's clever solution, a full-size bus pulled up. Plankton got off the bus, carrying two suitcases. "Well, it's great to be back!"

Then he noticed the tiny city of Bikini Bottom. Standing next to it, he looked like a giant.

"Huh?" he said.

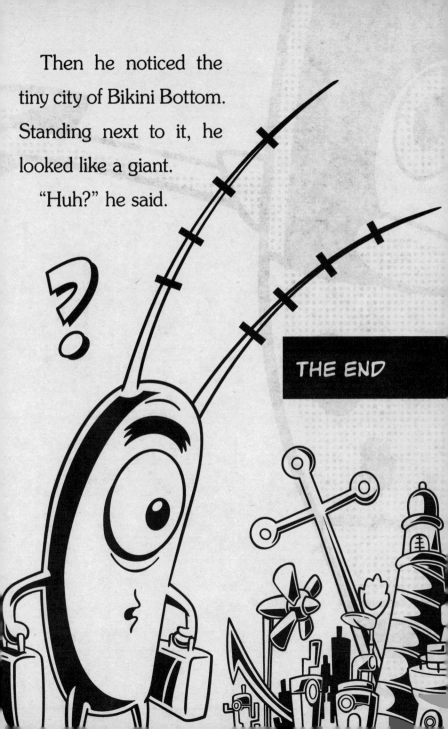

THE END

Then he noticed the
... of Silent Bob ...
... next to ...
...

"Huh?" he said.

E.V.I.L. VS. THE I.J.L.S.A.

By Erica David

DRIED UP

It was a beautiful morning in Bikini Bottom, but for SpongeBob SquarePants the night before had been downright ugly.

SpongeBob turned to his pet snail. "I had the worst nightmare, Gary!" he said, thinking back to his terrible dream. . . .

In the dream, SpongeBob and Patrick had been walking down the street dressed as their hero alter egos, Man Sponge and Boy Patrick. They were on the lookout for adventure. Suddenly, they noticed a jellyfish floating in the sky with a drawing taped to its side.

"Look, Pat!" Man Sponge said, pointing.

"Oh, pretty! It's a jellyfish wearing a picture of some cheese!" said Boy Patrick.

"That's not cheese! That's me! It's the Sponge Signal!" Man Sponge explained.

"That means there's trouble afoot and it's up to Man Sponge to save the day!"

"And Boy Patrick!" Patrick added. Then he scratched his head, confused. "Hey, SpongeBob, where's the Pat Signal?"

"Pat Signal? Don't be ridiculous. There isn't one," said Man Sponge. "Quickly, to the Sponge Lair!"

They ran off to the Sponge Lair—which looked a lot like SpongeBob's house. As soon as they walked in, they heard the phone ringing.

"I'll get it," Boy Patrick volunteered.

"Not so fast," Man Sponge said. He pointed to a sign stuck to the phone. "What does that say, my trusty sidekick?"

SPONGE PHONE

Boy Patrick peered at the sign. "Sponge Phone," he read.

"That's right. It's the *Sponge* Phone, not the *Pat* Phone. Kindly stand aside while I answer the call of justice." Man Sponge swept past Boy Patrick and picked up the phone.

"That's not fair," Boy Patrick grumbled, but Man Sponge didn't hear him. He was too busy answering the call of justice.

"Copy that, sir! We'll be there right away!" said Man Sponge, hanging up. "To the *Invisible Floatmobile*, Boy Patrick! Someone's in danger!"

The two action heroes raced outside and hopped into a rickety old boat.

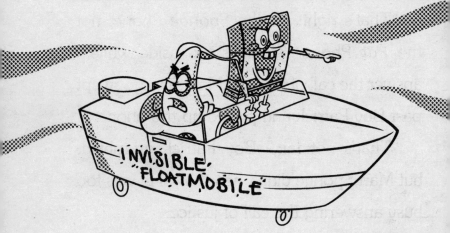

"Put the pedal to the metal, Boy Patrick! We've no time to lose!" cried Man Sponge from the passenger seat.

"But I drove *last* time," Boy Patrick complained.

"Right, you did, my crime-fighting companion. But I am Man Sponge and I must be free to keep an eye out for evil at all times."

"Somebody's getting a little too big for his superpants," Boy Patrick muttered.

A short while later, the *Invisible Floatmobile* screeched to a halt on a busy street in downtown Bikini Bottom.

"Look, over there! That citizen is in desperate need of a rescue!" Man Sponge exclaimed. He pointed to a young lady whose arms were piled high with packages.

"There's a puddle of mud in front of her and she's going to walk right through it!" Boy Patrick gasped. "We've got to help her!"

"I'll handle this, Boy Patrick!" said Man Sponge confidently. He scurried over to the puddle, flopped down on top of it, and soaked up the mud just as the young lady was about to step in it.

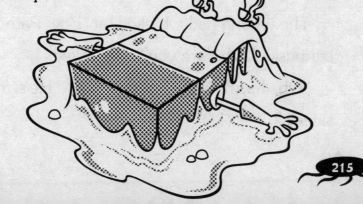

"My hero!" she cried and covered Man Sponge with kisses. "How will I ever repay you?"

"No payment necessary, ma'am. It's my duty to help citizens in need," Man Sponge told her, smiling.

"It's my duty, too," Boy Patrick added, hoping to win a kiss.

The young lady looked at Boy Patrick curiously. "Who are you?" she asked.

"Oh, him?" Man Sponge said. "He's my sidekick."

"Your sidekick? *Your* sidekick?!" Boy Patrick shouted angrily. "We're supposed to be a team! I'm tired of being your flunky, Man Sponge!"

Back in the present, SpongeBob shuddered. "It was such an awful dream, Gary! And it all seemed so real!"

"Meow," Gary replied.

"I know, Gary. Boy Patrick was so angry with me. I'm glad it was just a dream." SpongeBob breathed a sigh of relief.

"Meow!" Gary exclaimed.

"Goodness! You're right, Gary. Look at the time! I'd better get ready for work."

SpongeBob quickly took a shower, brushed his teeth, and got dressed. By the time he was ready to leave, he'd forgotten all about his bad dream. Whistling happily, he opened his front door and came face-to-face with Patrick.

"Hey there, buddy," SpongeBob greeted his friend.

But Patrick wasn't happy. He glared at SpongeBob and waved the picket sign he was holding. SpongeBob stared at the sign and gasped. It read: MAN SPONGE IS DRIED UP!

LATE FOR WORK

SpongeBob couldn't believe his eyes. He looked from Patrick to the sign, and back to Patrick again. "Gee, Pat, is that any way to treat your best friend?"

"I told you, SpongeBob. I'm tired of being your flunky!"

"My flunky? Now wait just a—" SpongeBob stopped. "Uh-oh, last night wasn't a dream, was it? It was real."

"Of course it was real!" Patrick bellowed.

"Listen, Pat—"

"No, you listen, SpongeBob. You think

that just because I'm your sidekick you can kick me around. Well I've had it! I'm tired of you taking all the glory!"

"Don't be silly, Pat. I don't take all the glory."

"Oh yeah? What about that time with the catfish?" Patrick's frown deepened as he thought back to that fateful day. . . .

Man Sponge and Boy Patrick were out patrolling the streets of Bikini Bottom when they heard a desperate cry for help.

"Help! Please, somebody help me!" a young woman cried tearfully. "It's my pet catfish. He's stuck in a patch of coral!"

Man Sponge and Boy Patrick rushed to the woman's side.

"Not to worry, lad. I'll help you," Man Sponge told her.

Boy Patrick looked at the catfish and noticed that it was scared. "Here, kitty. Here, kitty, kitty," he whispered, hoping to coax it free.

"Nice try, Boy Patrick, but that'll never work. A situation like this calls for a much more sophisticated approach," Man Sponge explained. He stared at the trapped catfish and scratched his chin in thought. "Aha! I've got it! Watch and learn."

Man Sponge knelt down next to the coral patch and whispered, "Here, kitty. Here, kitty, kitty."

Sure enough, the catfish swished its fins and worked its way free.

"You did it! You saved my catfish! Oh, thank you, Man Sponge!" said the young woman. "That was amazing!"

"It was pretty amazing, wasn't it? I don't know where I get these ideas. It's like they just come to me," Man Sponge replied. "Well, I've got to go, miss. Duty calls."

"Those were good times," SpongeBob said when Patrick was done remembering.

"Yeah, except for the part where you stole my idea and took all the glory!" Patrick snapped.

"Look, Pat, can we talk about this later?" SpongeBob asked. "I'm late for work."

"No, SpongeBob, I'm tired of being ignored. I won't wait!" Patrick said firmly.

"Well, neither will my customers! They depend on me for Krabby Patties!" SpongeBob argued.

"Then I guess you don't have a choice," Patrick grumbled.

The two friends stared angrily at each other. Exasperated, SpongeBob began walking toward the Krusty Krab. Patrick followed, waving his sign and chanting, "Down with Man Sponge!"

224

SECOND BANANA

When SpongeBob and Patrick walked up to the Krusty Krab, there was a long line of customers winding all the way down the block. *I wonder what's going on*, SpongeBob thought. He rushed inside with Patrick close on his heels.

At the front of the line were two very familiar heroes—Mermaidman and Barnacleboy! They were staring at the menu board in confusion.

"Let's see, I want a . . . no . . . I'll have a . . . no . . . hmmm . . ." Mermaidman mumbled uncertainly.

"Sir, will you please order already? You're holding up the line," Squidward said, annoyed. SpongeBob leaped at the chance to help his favorite heroes. He sidled up to Mermaidman and whispered, "Psst, Mermaidman, get a Krabby Patty!"

"I've made my decision!" Mermaidman announced.

The line of customers cheered. They'd been waiting forever for him to order.

"One Krabby Patty for me and one Pipsqueak Patty for the boy, please," said Mermaidman triumphantly.

"Now wait just a minute!" Barnacleboy stamped his foot in frustration. "I don't want a Pipsqueak Patty. I want an adult-size Krabby Patty."

"The Krabby Patty is too big for you," Mermaidman told him. "You'll never finish it all."

"The boy's eyes are bigger than his stomach," chuckled Mr. Krabs. The crowd of customers laughed, which only made Barnacleboy angrier.

"And that's another thing! I'm not a boy. I'm so old I've got hairs growing out of the wrinkles on my liver spots!" Barnacleboy snapped. But it didn't matter what he said.

Squidward ducked into the kitchen and came out holding the world's tiniest patty. "One Pipsqueak Patty and your bib and high chair," he said mockingly.

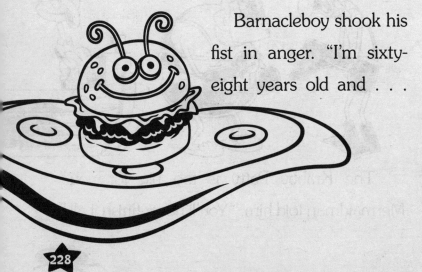

Barnacleboy shook his fist in anger. "I'm sixty-eight years old and . . .

I WANT A KRABBY PATTY!"

"Your Pipsqueak is getting cold," Mermaidman said gently. He picked up the tiny patty and held it out to his friend. "Shall I feed you?"

"Feed this, old man!" Barnacleboy shouted. He knocked the Pipsqueak Patty out of Mermaidman's hand.

"Ooooooo," the crowd gasped.

"I'm tired of playing second banana to you!" Barnacleboy yelled.

"But the two of you are a team! There's no such thing as second banana!" SpongeBob said. "Mermaidman and Barnacleboy work together to rid the world of evil! Remember the time Man Ray and the Dirty Bubble invented a dastardly Freeze Ray and threatened to put all of Bikini Bottom on ice?"

Barnacleboy folded his arms across his chest and sulked.

"Well, I do," SpongeBob said. "I remember it like it was yesterday . . ."

And with that SpongeBob told the crowd all about the amazing duo that once was Mermaidman and Barnacleboy. . . .

Mermaidman and Barnacleboy
were in hot pursuit of Man
Ray and the Dirty Bubble.

"Stop, in the name of
justice!" Mermaidman called after
the villains.

"Justice? I don't see anyone here by
that name," Man Ray snickered.

"Actually, Justice is my middle name," said
Barnacleboy.

"Does that mean we have to stop?" the
Dirty Bubble whispered to Man Ray.

"Keep moving," Man Ray said. "A few more
steps and we'll have them within position of
our Freeze Ray!"

"We've
got you now,
fiends!" cried
Mermaidman.

"Surrender or we'll— Do you hear that, Barnacleboy?"

"Hear what? This is no time to hesitate. Man Ray and the Dirty Bubble are about to escape!" said Barnacleboy.

Just then, an ice-cream truck rolled past playing a catchy little tune.

"Ice cream? I love ice cream!" Mermaidman exclaimed. He broke off from chasing the villains and ran after the ice-cream truck.

"So, you like ice cream, do you?" Man Ray snarled. "One blast from our Freeze Ray and all of Bikini Bottom will be on ice!"

The Dirty Bubble turned to Man Ray and whispered, "What are we going to do once the whole town is frozen?"

"Not sure yet, but we're villains, we'll figure it out," Man Ray replied. He switched on the Freeze Ray and turned it toward Mermaidman and the ice-cream truck.

"What are you waiting for?" asked the Dirty Bubble. "Fire away!"

"I can't," said Man Ray. "It has to heat up."

"It's a Freeze Ray and it has to heat up? Oh, for Neptune's sake!" The Dirty Bubble looked ready to burst.

"Do you have prune with bran sprinkles? It's my favorite. Keeps me regular," Mermaidman told the ice-cream truck driver.

"Put down that cone, Mermaidman! There's evil at work!" Barnacleboy shouted.

"*EVIL?*" Mermaidman bellowed. "I hate evil!"

"You sure do," said Barnacleboy. "Now, why don't you use that utility belt of yours and help us capture these criminals!"

"That's right, Barnacleboy!" Mermaidman punched a button on his utility belt and blasted Man Ray and the Dirty Bubble with his Small

Ray. The two villains shrank rapidly until they were no bigger than the tiniest plankton. Barnacleboy scooped them up in his hand and dropped them into his pocket.

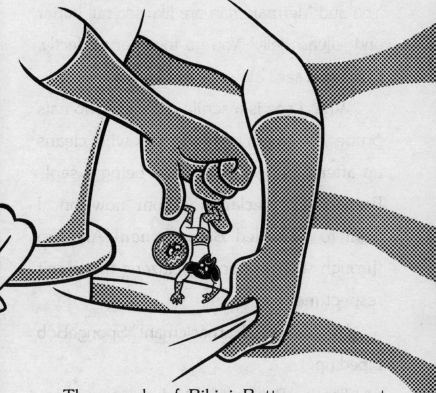

The people of Bikini Bottom came out of their houses and cheered, "Hooray for Mermaidman! Hooray for Barnacleboy!"

"Hooray!" SpongeBob said, getting caught up in his own memory. Back in the present he turned to Barnacleboy. "You never would have nabbed those villains without each other. You and Mermaidman are like sea-nut butter and jellyfish jelly! You go together perfectly. Don't you see?"

"What I see is a senile old man who eats prune ice cream and the sap who cleans up after him. Well, I'm done being a sap!" Barnacleboy declared. "From now on, I want to be called Barnacle*man*! And I'm through with protecting citizens that don't respect me!"

"*I* respect you, Barnacleman!" SpongeBob piped up.

"That's Barnacle*boy*! I mean, *man*. Ooooh, forget you people! I say, if you're not going to give me any respect as a hero, then maybe you'll give me respect as a villain!

A villain who is . . .

EVIL!"

Barnacleman roared.

Evil! SpongeBob gasped.

"Evil?" Mr. Krabs and Patrick cried in unison.

"EVIL?" Mermaidman bellowed.

"That's right! I'm crossing over to the dark side," Barnacleman announced. He pointed to the opposite side of the room. It was pitch black.

"What? Why should I waste money lighting the whole store?" Mr. Krabs asked sheepishly.

Suddenly, a sleek boatmobile cruised out of the darkness. The door slid open to reveal two of Bikini Bottom's most notorious criminals.

THE DARK SIDE

Man Ray poked his head out of the window, an evil grin forming on his face. "Did someone say *evil*?"

"I did!" Barnacleman answered. "As in, sign me up!"

"Holy oil spill! It's Mermaidman and Barnacleboy's archenemies, Man Ray and the Dirty Bubble!" SpongeBob exclaimed.

"Not so fast," said Man Ray. "The last time I checked, we were enemies."

"Archenemies," SpongeBob corrected him.

"Quite right, archenemies," Man Ray

agreed. "So why should we let you join us?"

"Well, he doesn't eat much," Squidward said dryly, "just a Pipsqueak Patty every now and then."

"I've had just about enough of your lip, mister!" Barnacleman growled at Squidward.

"Oooo, he's feisty. I say we take him," said the Dirty Bubble.

"You may be right, my filthy friend," Man Ray replied. "He might be a welcome addition to our plan for world domination, since the last plan didn't go so well."

Man Ray remembered the last time their efforts to rule the world failed. . . .

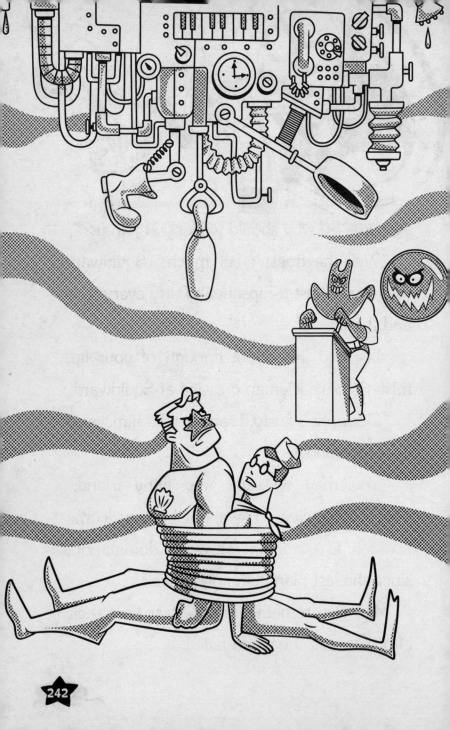

At long last Man Ray and the Dirty Bubble had Mermaidman and Barnacleboy in their clutches! The two heroic do-gooders were tied back-to-back. Above them loomed a mysterious contraption built of bowling pins, vacuum cleaner hoses, old shoes, rusty pipes, and various other odds and ends, casting a menacing shadow over the superduo.

"World domination here we come!" said Man Ray.

"I can't wait!" the Dirty Bubble replied. "I'm absolutely exhausted! Who knew mayhem could be so tiring! As soon as we rule the world I'm going on vacation."

"I hear the Indian Ocean is lovely this time of year," Man Ray suggested.

"Really? I was thinking the Bay of Biscay—"

"Sorry to interrupt," Mermaidman cut in, "but you're forgetting the one thing standing between you and your vacation."

"The rainy season? Oh, you're right. Last year the Atomic Flounder and I went to the Caribbean in the middle of July and almost got washed away! Never again!" the Dirty Bubble exclaimed.

"Not the rainy season! *Us!*" Mermaidman cried. "You'll have to go through us!"

"Yeah!" Barnacleboy seconded. He glanced up at the bizarre device that hung over them. "So your wicked plan is to . . . junk us into submission?"

"Junk? This isn't junk! What you see above you is a masterpiece!" Man Ray declared. "A brilliant display of criminal genius!"

"That's right!" said the Dirty Bubble. "Uh, how does it work again?" he asked Man Ray.

"Simple. I turn this crank here, which draws back the boot, which kicks the pipe, which rattles the cage, which knocks the pin that loosens the net, which drops from the hook, and falls on the clam that chews through the rope . . ."

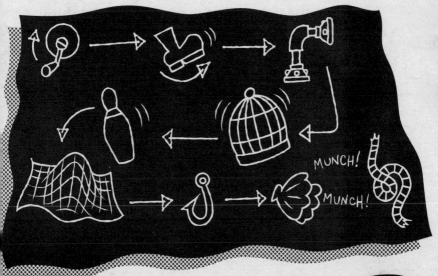

As Man Ray's explanation went on and on, Mermaidman and Barnacleboy tried to think of a way out. In an effort to free himself from the ropes around his arms, Barnacleboy accidentally elbowed Mermaidman in the side, which caused him to shout out in pain. This, then, reminded him that a shout was all it would take to free them both. "Sea creatures! UNITE!" he cried out.

The ocean rippled all around them. Man Ray was almost finished explaining his machine when a mass of fish, dolphins, clams, and sea horses swam toward them. The sea creatures nibbled through Mermaidman and Barnacleboy's ropes, freeing them.

"Thank you, friends!" said
Mermaidman. "Now, how'd you
like a closer look at a masterpiece?"
Following his command, the sea creatures
turned to Man Ray's machine. They bumped
and butted it with their bodies until it was
nothing more than a pile of rubble.

"Noooooooo!" Man Ray shouted.

"Foiled again!" cried the Dirty Bubble in
defeat.

Returning from his reverie, Man Ray concluded: "And we would have won if you could've controlled your limbs, Barnacleman!"

"All the more reason to have him on our side," the Dirty Bubble reminded his partner.

"Agreed. Welcome to Team E.V.I.L., Barnacleman," said Man Ray.

Barnacleman hopped into the villains' boat and sneered at Mermaidman. "Nighty night, you old goat!" He slammed the door and the boat sped off.

"Nighty night," Mermaidman replied. "Will you tuck me in?" he asked SpongeBob. Unfortunately, SpongeBob was too stunned to reply. The world's most famous crime-fighting team had just split up! It was too awful for words!

Then, things went from bad to worse.

"I'm joining the dark side, too," Patrick

announced. "Take that, Man Sponge!" He walked across the room and stood on the dark side of the restaurant.

Five seconds later . . .

"Um, it's dark over here," Patrick whined. "Anybody got a light?"

Squidward sighed in exasperation. "The villains left already, Patrick! It's too late to join them."

"Oh, right. I knew that." Patrick looked sheepish. He came back to the lit side of the restaurant and stood next to Mr. Krabs.

Moments later a voice rang out. "We interrupt your bleak and meaningless lives for this special news break!"

E.V.I.L.

SpongeBob, Patrick, Sandy, Squidward, and Mr. Krabs all looked up at the TV hanging over the front counter for a special news bulletin.

The news announcer continued, "Man Ray, the Dirty Bubble, and now playing for the dark side, Barnacleboy—"

"Barnacle*man*!" shouted Barnacleman from the TV screen.

"—have been committing a series of crimes throughout Bikini Bottom," the news

announcer explained.

SpongeBob watched the news footage in horror. Man Ray, the Dirty Bubble, and Barnacleman were wreaking havoc all over town. SpongeBob covered his eyes! He couldn't bear to look! But seconds later his curiosity got the best of him. He peeked through his fingers only to see the three criminals pull the worst prank of all. They ran up to a house, rang the doorbell, and then ran away!

"I'll get you crazy kids!" shouted the old man who answered the door.

The villains snickered as they ran off to cause more trouble.

Back at the news desk, the announcer continued. "These three criminals have named their new alliance Every Villain Is Lemons . . . otherwise known as E.V.I.L.! What can we do?

When will this crime wave end? How will we defeat the evil? Why am I asking you all these questions? Mermaidman, where are you?"

Mermaidman had dozed off. Mr. Krabs swatted him with a claw, jolting him awake. "I'm right here!" said Mermaidman. "Don't worry, good citizens! Nothing will stop me from defeating evil . . . nothing!"

Mermaidman ran out of the Krusty Krab hot on the trail of evil. Suddenly, he heard a familiar sound. An ice-cream truck rolled into view.

"Ice cream! I love ice cream!" he said, forgetting all about evil. "A double scoop of prune with bran sprinkles!"

A mysterious gloved hand snaked out from the window and handed Mermaidman his ice-cream cone.

Mermaidman took one lick and the cone exploded. "Goes right through me every time," he said, stunned.

Just then, he heard an evil laugh.

Barnacleman leaned out of the ice-cream truck with Man Ray and the Dirty Bubble at his side. "You might as well give it up, old man. There are three of us and only one of you. You don't stand a chance!" Barnacleman gloated. He took the wheel of the ice-cream truck and drove off, tires squealing.

"Mermaidman, are you all right?" SpongeBob asked as he came running up.

Patrick, Sandy, and Squidward were right behind him. "Oh, how are you going to beat all three of those guys by yourself?"

Mermaidman's shoulders slumped. "You're right. I give up." He flopped down on the ground.

"You can't give up! What if we help you?" SpongeBob suggested.

"That's a terrible idea," Mermaidman said grumpily. "Wait, I've got it!" He snapped his fingers. "What if you help me?"

"Okay," SpongeBob agreed.

"So, who wants to save the world?" Mermaidman asked.

"I do!" SpongeBob answered eagerly.

"I do!" said Sandy.

"I do!" Patrick cried.

"I don't," Squidward grumbled.

"Oh, yes you do!" said Mr. Krabs as he scuttled up to them. "No world means no money." He told Squidward. "Now go save the world or you're fired."

"That's settled then," said Mermaidman brightly. "To the Mermalair!"

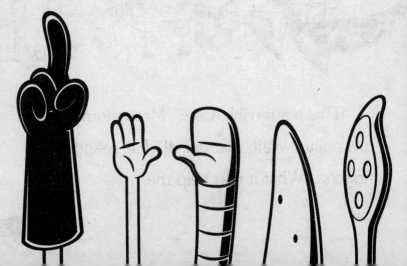

THE P.J.L.S.A.

"Wow, the Mermalair!" SpongeBob marveled, as he, Patrick, Sandy, and Squidward followed Mermaidman into the headquarters of Bikini Bottom's most famous action heroes. It was full of crime-fighting gadgets, inventions, and devices—not to mention the smell of justice wafting through its halls.

They walked past a row of costumes, each one enclosed in its own glass case.

"These costumes belong to the original International Justice League of Super Acquaintances," explained Mermaidman.

"Wow! The I.J.L.S.A. were the most heroic heroes ever! And you had the best lunch box, too," SpongeBob said to Mermaidman.

"The I.J.L.S.A. did more than just look good on a lunch box. We were an unstoppable team of crime-fighting equals!"

"Equals?" Patrick perked up. "You mean, like nobody was a flunky?"

"That's right, Peter," Mermaidman replied.

"And you all took turns driving the boatmobile?" asked Patrick. He cut SpongeBob a knowing look.

"Right again, Pedro! We were a team," said Mermaidman. "Why, I remember this one time . . ."

Mermaidman thought back to the famous bank heist that the I.J.L.S.A. had thwarted. . . .

Mermaidman and his fellow Super Acquaintances—the Quickster, Captain Magma, the Elastic Waistband, and Miss Appear—were all gathered at the Mermalair when the phone rang.

"I'll get it," said Mermaidman, picking up the receiver. "Hello? Oh, hey there, chief. What's that you say? A robbery? Not to worry! We'll be right there!" Mermaidman hung up. "Super Acquaintances, to the *Invisible Boatmobile!*"

The superfriends ran through the Mermalair to the secret cavern where they kept their boat. Mermaidman was the first to arrive. He unlocked the *Invisible Boatmobile* and held open the door for his crime-fighting companions. "After you," he said.

"No, after you," said the Quickster.

"No, after you," Mermaidman replied.

"Really, I insist," the Quickster said.

"Don't be silly, we're all equals here," Mermaidman pointed out.

"Then ladies first," the Quickster said to Miss Appear.

"Oh no, I couldn't," Miss Appear replied. "After you, Captain Magma."

"I think the Waistband should go first," Captain Magma said.

"No, after you," said the Elastic Waistband.

Five minutes later, the Super Acquaintances

had finally piled into the *Invisible Boatmobile*. They took off, headed for Bikini Bottom National Bank.

When they got to the scene, they saw two criminals running out of the bank with bags of money.

"I'll stop them!" cried Mermaidman. "Unless you want to, Waistband."

"No, no," said the Elastic Waistband. "You go right ahead."

"Are you sure?" asked Mermaidman.

"I'm positive. Unless it's Magma's turn."

"I just thwarted a crime yesterday," Captain Magma replied. "Really, it's up to the Quickster to keep our streets safe."

"I wouldn't feel right," said the Quickster. "Not when Miss Appear is just as worthy as I am."

"Oh, stop your sweet talk, Quickster." Miss Appear chuckled.

"Well, someone needs to stop them!" cried an innocent bystander.

"You're right!" said Mermaidman. "Super Acquaintances, unite!"

The Quickster used his superspeed to run circles around the thieves. He ran so fast that he made them dizzy.

Next, Miss Appear turned herself invisible. She sneaked up to the dizzy bandits and slipped the money bags out of their hands. They never even saw her coming!

"What's going on?" asked the first villain, scared.

"I don't know," his partner in crime answered. "Forget the money! Let's get out of here, man."

The criminals made a break for it, but Mermaidman pelted them with water balls. Then, the Elastic Waistband used his amazing powers of elasticity to stretch himself into a long, thin rope. He wrapped himself around the criminals and kept them tied up until the police arrived.

Once again, the Super Acquaintances had saved the day!

"That's incredible!" said SpongeBob when Mermaidman had finished his story.

"It sure is," Mermaidman agreed. "And now I'm giving you the chance to join me and form a new league of Super Acquaintances!" He touched a button and lowered the glass cases surrounding the costumes. "Now, who's with me?"

KRACK-A-TOWA!

SpongeBob shot Patrick a nervous glance. "Just a second, Mermaidman," he said, pulling Patrick aside.

"What are we going to do?" SpongeBob whispered urgently to Patrick. "This is our chance to be part of a legendary team of crime-fighters!"

"Yeah, a real team of equals!" Patrick said dreamily.

"But what about Man Sponge and Boy Patrick?"

"What about them?" Patrick asked.

"If we put on these costumes we'll have to give them up. We can't be both!"

Patrick frowned. "I hadn't thought about that."

"It's true, Patrick! What are we going to do? I can't just stop being Man Sponge. Remember the day we first became super crime-fighters?"

"Like it was yesterday," Patrick replied. "It all started when you were bit by the rabid clam."

"Huh?" SpongeBob said.

"You know, that rabid clam. We thought something

was wrong with it 'cause it was glowing in the dark. Then it just hopped up and snapped you right on the nose."

"Patrick, that's not how it—"

"Then the next day you started to feel funny, and that's when you discovered your special powers, like the power to see real good and the power to make Krabby Patties—"

"Patrick—"

"'From this day forth, I shall call myself Man Sponge,' you said. 'Huzzah!'"

SpongeBob thought about interrupting again, but decided against it. Patrick was on a roll.

"Then there was the birth of Boy Patrick, who came to earth in a meteor shower as a tiny baby," Patrick said. "He was raised in

a small farm town outside of Bikini Bottom and draws his powers from the Dutchman's golden spatula!"

"WHOSOEVER HOLDS THIS SPATULA, HE BE WORTHY, SHALL POSSESS THE POWER OF... THE DUTCHMAN"

"Patrick!" SpongeBob couldn't contain himself any longer. "That's not what happened!"

"It's not?"

"No, I think you're confusing us with other heroes."

"I am?"

"Yes."

"Then what really happened?" asked Patrick.

"Well, we were going to go jellyfishing but we found holes in our nets, remember? So we decided to do arts and crafts at my house," SpongeBob explained.

"And that's when the rabid clam bit you!" Patrick gasped.

"No, Pat. There was no rabid clam. We made masks out of construction paper and spent the afternoon picking out super names."

"That's it?" Patrick asked.

SpongeBob nodded, tears welling at the corners of his eyes as he thought about that special day.

"If you two are done strolling down memory lane, I'd like to get this show on the road," Mermaidman said. "It's almost time for my nap."

"What do we have to do?" SpongeBob looked anxious.

"Just put on these costumes and the fantastic powers of the International Justice League of Super Acquaintances will become yours!" Mermaidman explained.

"Wow! I didn't think superpowers worked that way," Sandy said.

"Sure. The power is all in the costume," Mermaidman told them. "Why else would we run around in colored undies?"

"Wait a minute," said SpongeBob. "You

mean these costumes come with *real* superpowers?"

"That's right, Bucky," Mermaidman replied.

SpongeBob and Patrick exchanged a glance. They could still be Man Sponge and Boy Patrick when they switched costumes. "Count us in!" they said together.

"Excellent!" cried Mermaidman. "Let's get everyone into their outfits."

A short while later, the new I.J.L.S.A. emerged wearing their costumes. SpongeBob was absolutely thrilled. He imagined the news reporting on this momentous event. . . .

"Breaking news!" said the imaginary announcer. "We go live to the Mermalair, where a new International Justice League of Super Acquaintances has just been formed. Here they are now!"

SpongeBob waved to the imaginary camera in his shiny Quickster uniform.

"The Quickster! With the uncanny ability to run really quick!" said the newscaster.

"Want to see me run to that mountain and back?" SpongeBob asked. He moved so quickly it looked like he was standing still.

"Captain Magma! Get him angry and he's bound to erupt!" announced the newscaster.

"KRACK-A-TOWA!"

Squidward shouted, shooting flames from Magma's fiery helmet.

"The Elastic Waistband," the newscaster cried, "able to stretch his body into fantastic shapes and forms!"

"I can finally touch my toes!" Patrick exclaimed, using the waistband's powers to twist himself into a pretzel.

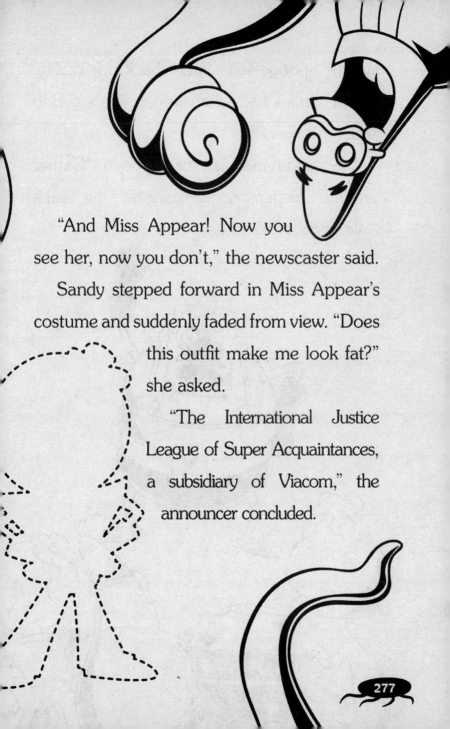

"And Miss Appear! Now you see her, now you don't," the newscaster said. Sandy stepped forward in Miss Appear's costume and suddenly faded from view. "Does this outfit make me look fat?" she asked.

"The International Justice League of Super Acquaintances, a subsidiary of Viacom," the announcer concluded.

When SpongeBob came back to reality, Mermaidman had fallen asleep. SpongeBob shook him gently.

Mermaidman's eyes sprang open. "Gather around, Super Acquaintances," he said. "We've got work to do."

MAKE-OUT REEF

Later at the Mermalair, the I.J.L.S.A. was in the middle of some very important business.

"So it's agreed," Mermaidman said, "we'll get one cheese pizza, one with pepperoni and mushrooms, and one with olives."

Suddenly, the video screen on the wall lit up.

"Super Acquaintances, we need your help!" someone cried.

"Holy halibut! It's the chief!" the Quickster said.

"Thank you for the introduction, Quickster,

but we all know who I am. More to the point, we've got news on the whereabouts of E.V.I.L.," the chief explained.

"The whoseabouts of what?" asked the Elastic Waistband.

"You just tell us where they are, chief, and we'll hootie 'em faster than you can say 'salsa verde,'" Miss Appear promised.

"Our sources last saw E.V.I.L. harassing some teenagers up at Make-Out Reef! You know, Make-Out Reef. Woo-hoo! Mwah! Mwah!" said the chief, making kissing noises.

"Floppin' flounder, Mermaidman! Make-Out Reef!" The Quickster gasped.

"Those fiends!" cried Mermaidman.

"Ah, Make-Out Reef! Good times, good times." Captain Magma chuckled softly to himself.

"To Make-Out Reef! AWAY!" called Mermaidman.

"Does this mean we're not getting pizza?" the Elastic Waistband asked sadly.

Meanwhile, at Make-Out Reef, the super villains known as E.V.I.L. were doing their best to pester teenagers.

Man Ray, the Dirty Bubble, and Barnacleman taunted a pair of teenagers parked in a boat. "John and Nancy sittin' in a tree, K-I-S-S-I-N-G!" they chanted, shining a flashlight on them.

"Leave us alone!" the young couple cried. The villains laughed mischievously.

"Shine the flashlight in that car over there, Man Ray!" the Dirty Bubble urged his partner in crime.

"With pleasure," Man Ray replied. He shined the flashlight on another parked car. The light revealed a lonely boy inside kissing a pillow.

"Hey, man, that's not cool," the boy complained.

The three criminals snickered. They hadn't had this much fun in ages!

Just then, Mermaidman arrived to put an end to their laughter. "Leave those young kids alone!" he cried.

"Well, if it isn't Milkmaidman. You saved us the trouble of tracking you down," Man Ray hissed.

"You fiends can't win. You're outnumbered!" Mermaidman shouted.

"You senile bag of fish paste! There are three of us and only one of you," Man Ray growled.

"Make that two!" called the Quickster as he raced to Mermaidman's side.

"Three!" Captain Magma rocketed onto the scene.

"Four!" The Elastic Waistband stretched to join his friends.

"Five!" cried Miss Appear, suddenly visible.

"And me makes ten," Mermaidman said, counting on his fingers. "I think."

"Uh-oh, I don't feel so good about this," the Dirty Bubble said nervously. In fact, all three supervillains looked worried.

"Well, there goes our big toy deal!" Barnacleman sighed.

"Super Acquaintances, attack!" Mermaidman shouted.

"No! Please! Mercy!" cried Barnacleman. He and the alliance of E.V.I.L. were quaking in their boots.

"Krack-a-towa!" Captain Magma shouted. A burst of flaming lava shot out from the top of his fiery helmet. Unfortunately, instead of landing on the criminals, it plopped down on top of the Quickster's head.

"AHHHHH! AHHHH! GET IT OFF! GET IT OFF! GET IT OFF!"

the Quickster screamed. Panicked, he ran in a circle trying to shake off the burning lava.

"I'll save you, Quickster!" said the Elastic Waistband. He took off after his friend. What happened next wasn't pretty. The Quickster was moving really fast—so fast that the Elastic Waistband's rubbery arms and legs got tangled up in his wake.

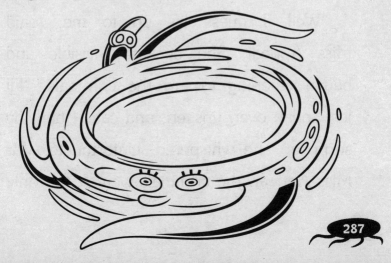

"I'll cool you off, Quickster, with one of my water balls!" Mermaidman said. By this time the Quickster was running so fast he was a blur. Mermaidman squinted trying to see him. He launched a water ball, but it accidentally landed on Captain Magma instead.

"Noooo!" Captain Magma cried, as the water ball doused his flames and reduced him to ashes.

"Well, I guess it's up to me," said Miss Appear. She became invisible and began creeping toward the criminals. "I'll just sneak over, unseen, and catch them by surprise," she whispered. Unfortunately for Miss Appear, the criminals weren't the only ones who couldn't see her. Suddenly, she was hit by a passing boat and knocked off a cliff! The driver had no idea she was there!

"Get it off! Get it off!" The Quickster was still aflame and running in circles. At last the lava burned out, but there was nothing left of the Quickster except two smoking shoes.

Mermaidman took one look at the sad state of the Super Acquaintances and fell over.

Man Ray, the Dirty Bubble, and Barnacleman stared at one another in shock. They had gone from being outnumbered to defeating a legendary crime-fighting team without lifting a finger.

"We did it! We won! The day belongs to E.V.I.L.!" Barnacleman said triumphantly.

UH, WORLD DOMINATION?

Barnacleman gloated. "Heh, heh, heh! You've lost, Mermaidman. And the hero-villain rules say you have to give in to my demands."

Mermaidman knelt down in front of Barnacleman. "Okay, what do you want?"

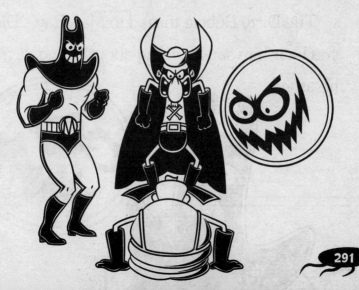

"World domination! Tell him we want world domination!" Man Ray said eagerly.

"And make him eat dirt!" the Dirty Bubble added.

"Number one: I want to be treated like an equal, not a sidekick," Barnacleman began. "Number two: I want to be called Barnacleman. And number three . . ."

"Come on, world domination!" Man Ray chimed in, fingers crossed.

"I want an adult-size Krabby Patty," Barnacleman finished.

The Dirty Bubble turned to Man Ray. "Did you hear him say anything about eating dirt?" he asked.

Mermaidman nodded, accepting the demands.

Barnacleman smiled. "Need a hand, Super Pal?" He reached out to Mermaidman and helped him get to his feet.

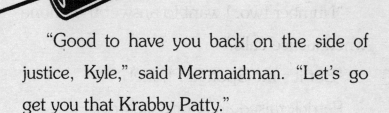

"Good to have you back on the side of justice, Kyle," said Mermaidman. "Let's go get you that Krabby Patty."

"Was that it?" asked Man Ray, thoroughly disappointed.

"No." Man Ray heard an unexpected voice. In his torn Elastic Waistband costume, Patrick gathered up his rubbery limbs and dragged them over to SpongeBob. "I've got some demands too."

"Oh, goody!" said the Dirty Bubble.

"Is it even worth me saying world domination again?" Man Ray asked dryly.

SpongeBob shook off the ashes of his Quickster outfit. "What do you want, Pat?"

"Well, number one: I don't want to always drive the *Invisible Floatmobile*," Patrick said.

"Okay, we'll take turns," SpongeBob agreed.

"Number two: I want to answer the phone when justice calls."

"But it's the Sponge Phone!"

Patrick raised an angry eyebrow.

"Fine," SpongeBob said. "I guess we can call it the Sponge–Pat Phone."

Patrick nodded. "And number three: Now that I've seen what it's like to be on a team of equals, no more second banana."

"Pat, you were never second banana.

I'm sorry if the whole superduo thing kinda went to my head. But I know I couldn't do it without you. We're a team! We go together like . . ."

"Sea-nut butter and jellyfish jelly?" Barnacleman suggested.

"Just like sea-nut butter and jellyfish jelly!" SpongeBob said. "Friends?" He reached out a hand to Patrick.

"Friends," Patrick agreed. He shook SpongeBob's hand and pulled him into a bear hug.

"Oh, for Neptune's sake!" cried Man Ray. "Will no one demand world domination?"

OH, PIPSQUEAK!

Later at the Krusty Krab, Mermaidman and Barnacleman were once again standing at the front of the line. This time, though, they knew exactly what to order.

"That'll be two Krabby Patties, please," said Mermaidman. "One for me and one for my . . . equal."

SpongeBob and Patrick watched as the two legendary crime-fighters carried their Krabby Patties to a table and sat down to eat lunch together.

"It does me good to see those two back

together again," said SpongeBob.

"Me too," Patrick replied.

"But there is one thing I'm kinda sad about."

"What's that?"

SpongeBob leaned forward and whispered, "I really miss being the Quickster."

"I know!" Patrick agreed.

"When I was the Waistband, I got to be all rubbery."

"I mean, Man Sponge is the greatest, but he's not as fast as the Quickster. No one is," SpongeBob said with a glint in his eye. "Those superpowers were *real*."

Patrick nodded. "Who knew they came with the costume? I always thought you had to get bitten by a rabid clam."

"Well, I guess we just have to settle for what we have," SpongeBob said sadly.

"Maybe not," Patrick replied. "Maybe we can make up our own superpowers."

"Patrick! That's a brilliant idea!"

"Oooo, I know what mine is," Patrick said. "I have the power to sleep with my eyes open!"

"And I, Man Sponge, am the world's best trash picker-upper!" SpongeBob announced.

"I think it's time for us to test out our new superpowers. To the Sponge Lair, AWAY!"

SpongeBob and Patrick dashed across the restaurant. On their way out they heard their favorite heroes deep in conversation.

"How's that adult-size Krabby Patty treating you, Barnacleman?" Mermaidman asked.

"Actually, it's pretty big. I'm not sure I can finish the whole thing," Barnacleman replied.

Mermaidman stared at his friend for a moment and then burst out laughing. Barnacleman laughed, too. It wasn't long before the whole restaurant was laughing with them, remembering the Pipsqueak Patty that started it all.

THE END